VARFELIS STATION

OPERATION MARRAKESH
BOOK 3

BLAZE WARD

KNOTTED ROAD PRESS

Varfelis Station
Operation Marrakesh, Book 3
Blaze Ward
Copyright © 2024 Blaze Ward
All rights reserved
Published by Knotted Road Press
www.KnottedRoadPress.com

ISBN: 978-1-64470-500-1

Cover art:
Illustration 52629036 © Lostflower | Dreamstime.com

Cover and interior design copyright © 2024 Knotted Road Press

Reviews
It's true. Reviews help. Even a short one, such as, "Loved it!" So please consider reviewing this book (and all of the ones you've read) on your favorite retailer site.

Never miss a release!
If you'd like to be notified of new releases, sign up for my newsletter.

http://www.blazeward.com/newsletter/

Buy More!
Did you know that you can buy directly from the Knotted Road Press website?

https://www.knottedroadpress.com/shop/

ALSO BY BLAZE WARD

The Jessica Keller Chronicles

Auberon

Queen of the Pirates

Last of the Immortals

Goddess of War

Flight of the Blackbird

The Red Admiral

St. Legier

Winterhome

Petron

CS-405

Queen Anne's Revenge

Packmule

Persephone

First Centurion Kosnett

Encounter at Vilahana

Consensus at Aditi

Hegemony at Dalou

Princes at Ewin

Empire at Gloran

Domain at Yaumgan

Additional Alexandria Station Stories

The Story Road

Siren

Two Bottles of Wine With A War God

The Science Officer Series Season One

The Science Officer

The Mind Field

The Gilded Cage

The Pleasure Dome

The Doomsday Vault

The Last Flagship

The Hammerfield Gambit

The Hammerfield Payoff

The Bryce Connection

The Science Officer Series Season Two

Alien Seas

Buried Among the Stars

Captain Navarre

Last Stand

Lost Dreams

Ghost Towns

Games People Play

Prophet and Loss

Dandelion

Emergency

Warchild

Moot

Doomsday Girl

Princess

The Coven

Preacher Man

Captain Daring

Revoked

PRELUDE

Log: Directorate Cruiser, Tactical Transport
  Marrakesh (CTT)
Station: Horwin
Attached Special Mission Modules:
A) Q-Module
B) Gas Transport
Mission: Scouting and Resupply
Project: Q73-F7J23L99
Security Clearance: 5+

1

———

Padraig studied the waiting room. They were back on Horwin, the capital world of the *Sovereign Collective Directorate of A'Zedi*.

Home, though not his. Padraig was originally from Mancastre.

And this building was not part of the Ministry of War. As an *A'Zedi* sailor, and a captain to boot, he'd spent most of his adult life either in War Ministry offices or aboard warships. Today, he was in a place he *thought* belonged to *A'Zedi Intelligence Services*. Nobody would confirm nor deny.

Sitting next to him, also in her best dress uniform, Squire Nyssa Taggart was working on not fidgeting. Doing a pretty good job of it. The man in the civilian suit behind the counter across the way probably couldn't see how nervous she was, but Padraig was her commanding officer.

He could tell.

But then, she was barely twenty years old. She'd enlisted at seventeen, gone to Communications School where they'd discovered how brilliant the young woman was, and commissioned her. Fourth or fifth youngest crew member on his ship. Youngest officer by far.

He smiled at her.

"You're doing fine, Taggart," he offered quietly.

She smiled. Some.

The door behind the counter opened and a woman appeared.

"Captain, Squire, could you join me, please?" she asked.

As if there was any question.

Padraig rose and tugged everything into place. Nyssa did the same, then followed him into the inner office.

Mariami Gelashvili, Permanent First Secretary, *A'Zedi Intelligence Services*. Civilian spies, when Padraig and his Squire were both military.

But the *Orders to Report* had been extremely specific. Here. Now. Them. Done.

He went to the seat on the left and stood. Nyssa stood beside him.

"Please, be seated," Madam Gelashvili said as she moved around behind the desk and did the same.

It was a large desk. Dark-stained oak from the look. Polished surface with a small name placard to remind you who reigned here, and a holder with a pen. No electronics visible. No art on the wall behind her or to either side.

Madame Gelashvili was a tall, heavy-set woman who looked to be in her mid-fifties. Hair dyed a golden-brown with reddish tones underneath, and hazel eyes, both of which were fairly rare in *A'Zedi*. Reasonably pale skin, compared to most of *A'Zedi*, as well.

Padraig's darker skin and black hair was the most common around here. Nyssa Taggart was a bit darker than him in both, but not much.

Gelashvili looked more like someone from the *United Technocracy of Wronlori*, which, he supposed, made a bit of sense, if she'd really been a spy when she'd been younger.

They studied each other for a long moment before the woman spoke.

"Normally," she began without any prologue, "the Bureau of Personnel wouldn't have made such a mistake as putting you aboard an old Tactical Transport, Captain Boru. However, in reviewing the records, we have found a few places where the process could be made better in the future. For now, it is my fortuitous luck that an officer of your quality was already available in a position such as this. Additionally, that you have such an excellent crew."

"Ma'am?" Padraig replied, uncertain what she was looking for. But she had stopped to invite a comment. He simply didn't know what to inject.

"You should have gotten one of the newer cruisers, Boru," she said simply, smiling compactly. "Where, unfortunately, you'd have been assigned to a patrol squadron to punch numbers and billets unless and until something interesting happened."

He nodded. Line command was frequently like that. In peacetime, he might have gone off on show-the-flag missions or explorations, but *A'Zedi* was at war with *Wronlori*. Again. Or still. A Cruiser-Tactical-Transport didn't rate that important.

"Instead, you have accomplished a pair of missions that frankly should have both failed, Captain," she continued with a larger smile. "And when the Bureau considered transferring you to a newer warship, we stepped in."

There. Mousetrap.

Marrakesh's first mission, after being recommissioned from the storage yard with a brand-new crew and ink-not-yet-dry-on-promotion-papers Captain, had been to haul a bunch of experimental weapons out to the back of beyond, where they could be tested. And where a *Wronlori* Leviathan named *Sundering Wrath* had tried to kill them.

After repairs, it had been a diplomatic run to the galactic interior, where a murder mystery had nearly gotten him killed, too.

"How can I—we—serve, ma'am?" Padraig asked, nodding to Nyssa beside him.

She'd been ordered to accompany him, which took the situation out of merely weird and down into completely bizarre.

Naval bureaucracies didn't work that way.

"We would like to offer you a different mission, Captain, Squire," she said with a nod. "I've asked for both of you because of Squire Taggart's reports from Monsanch. The Agency was surprised at what you'd done, Squire Taggart. In a good way."

"What mission, Madam Secretary?" Padraig pressed.

He was a sailor. Promoted from Knight to Commander to Captain in just over a month, so as to take command of a worn-out Tactical Transport and get it refurbished for the new war, after the surprise attack against Eworn just about three years ago. Many years sooner than he should have made Captain, as he was one of the youngest he knew of. If not the youngest.

"You will still officially report to the Ministry of War, Captain," she told him. "They will continue to handle the basic things. Most of your crew will be none the wiser. However, we would like to use you and the Squire to undertake certain missions for *A'Zedi Intelligence Services*. Less time on the front line. Fewer missions merely hauling supplies from station to resupply base. More things related to espionage and such. What you have been doing previously, however accidentally, but with a more specific purpose."

"And my purpose in this meeting, ma'am?" Nyssa asked carefully.

She was the wild card, and they both knew it.

"Frankly, my experts didn't think that it was possible to crack those codes, Squire," Gelashvili smiled. "They'd like to train you some more, offer you better tools, and see what else you can do. But to do it in the field, rather than being in some office cubical somewhere."

Padraig liked the gobsmacked look on Nyssa's face. Matched his insides, because he'd kept his eyes cool and collected.

In spite of wanting to shriek.

"More dangerous, ma'am?" he asked her.

"Probably," she nodded. "However, you have shown yourself to be far more resourceful than our files would have originally suggested, Captain. And *Marrakesh*, with proper preparation, is still an *A'Zedi* warship."

Padraig considered it. Not much to think about, really. He was already serving, so it came down to how to best do that. If they wanted to use him and *Marrakesh* to further the war effort, that was why he'd signed up in the first place.

He nodded.

"What are your orders, ma'am?" he asked.

Gelashvili smiled.

"Let us talk about the Varfelis system, Captain."

Padraig was on his bridge. Seated in his chair. He didn't want to say he was superstitious, but he also wasn't going to deny that he felt better, sitting here.

Commander Chance Messier was aft on the Secondary Bridge with her team. He had Nyssa forward with him. Her station had been gutted during the most recent station visit, and all new hardware installed.

Outwardly, no change, but she'd assured him that it had doubled her reach and vastly multiplied her ability to take apart any but the most complex codes. Front-line military stuff was probably beyond her today, but the government wasn't sending *Marrakesh* out to engage *Wronlori* directly.

This time, it would be a civilian station. Or pirates. Folks back home weren't all that certain.

"Radio, what's showing on your boards?" Padraig asked.

New system, new mission. He had made sure that he had his entire first team on duty today, instead of rotating folks through watches. Assuming everything went well, they'd be back to normal tomorrow.

He wanted his best today.

"Not much, sir," Nyssa replied, keying and tapping. "Aetherial sensors show a handful of ships moving around, mostly at slow FTL speeds. Some look large, but our notes suggest those to be bulk cargo carriers rather than warships."

Padraig nodded. Varfelis was a long ways from any *A'Zedi* system. Middle of nowhere. It had one advantage of galactic geography in that Varfelis formed the point of an isosceles triangle, with *A'Zedi* and *Wronlori* as the base. Slightly closer to *A'Zedi* space, but still spinward and coreward enough to be out of the way.

Well out of the way.

Marrakesh was scouting. Varfelis wasn't on the way for a fleet making an attack one way or the other, but it was a nice space to put a refueling depot if you wanted to sneak someone around the long way and come up behind someone on your Ghostdrives.

He dialed a number on his armrest.

"Stevedore," Kaitlin replied instantly.

"How are your modules doing?" Padraig asked.

Marrakesh was a Tactical Transport. A cruiser hull with two big bays aft where huge modules could be plugged and changed as missions changed. It gave them a lot of flexibility in the field, assuming they were prepared.

"Gas transport module is empty, and all signs are green," Kaitlin replied. "Q Module crew are a little bored and hoping you'll give them something to shoot at soon."

"No promises," Padraig laughed. "If all goes well, I'll never need them to unmask in the first place."

"Understood," Kaitlin laughed back. "But you'll have to convince them yourself."

"Very good." He cut the line.

Q Module. Looked like a cargo pod, until you opened up a series of panels and suddenly had several missile racks, extra particle beam turrets, and a spare railgun installation for defense.

More firepower than the average cruiser, though less than a Ship of the Line. And more fragile, if you got into combat.

Q-ships were designed to lull the bad guys into getting too close, then overwhelming them with a wave of missiles.

He had this module because nobody knew what to expect in this region of space. *Unaffiliated* officially, which meant that no major nation claimed Varfelis. Not even an inhabitable planet ahead of them. At least, not according to the most recent records. Which were not even remotely recent.

Marrakesh was here to update things. And scout around.

"Helm, what's your status?" he asked.

Squire Zarah Halloran was piloting today. She'd been with him at Monsanch, down on the ground. Good officer, though she liked to joke that she was three days out of Uni. She had been when he'd first gotten her, but she was coming along nicely. Not as calm and competent as Taggart, but not many were.

"We'll drop into system in about twenty minutes, Captain," Halloran replied. "Confirming that our target is the inner edge of the snowball zone, sir?"

"That's right, Helm," he said. "We know that the inner planets are uninhabited and known to the locals as the Iron Zone. Three big gas giants outside that. Two ice giants beyond that. What we don't know for certain is if there are orbital periods of anything. All records are twenty to fifty years out of date at this point."

"We have a reasonable expectation of where they are, sir," Halloran replied. "Permission to aim for the outermost ice giant?"

Padraig considered it.

The mission was scouting and exploration. And nobody would believe that an *A'Zedi* warship, even a Tactical Transport like *Marrakesh*, was just out for a sail. Thus, the gas transport module. They could sail into low orbit of one of the giants, then drop a long dredge line deeper and vacuum up various exotic things to sell at the factory station orbiting the innermost gas giant, a monstrous world known as Sybeth with several dozen moons of various sizes around it.

"Go ahead," Padraig said.

All of this mission was playing it by ear. Gelashvili had told him that improvisation would be his most common need in a job like this, and that his successes at Albany and Monsanch had convinced them that he could.

Now, he just had to figure out what that meant.

And what it looked like.

He could do this.

3

———

"All hands, stand by to drop out of Ghost-space," Padraig called over the intercom. "We'll be emerging near the ice giant Ecix and scouting."

So far, so good.

"Halloran, as you bear," he called.

"Stand by," she replied. "Dropping in fifteen seconds."

Padraig didn't like to think of it as a combat insertion, but he'd gone ahead and brought the ship to alert anyway. A good training exercise, if nothing else.

Maddox Nevin was on Guns. Everyone else was wound that little extra bit tight today.

Then they dropped into realspace. Padraig didn't feel any difference as the Ghostdrives shut down, but all of his screens suddenly filled with data as Nyssa's sensors were back in their normal universe.

"Captain, you need to hear this," Nyssa called after a few seconds.

She keyed a switch on her console and a voice filled the bridge.

"-two-seven-three. Repeating, we are under attack by pirate vessels. Can anyone help? Orbiting Ecix and under attack by pirates. Please assist."

He turned to Zarah Halloran, sitting immediately next to Nyssa.

"Where are they?" he asked simply.

"We're almost on top of them, sir," she replied. "Those coordinates are about one hundred and forty degrees ahead of us in orbit, low on the horizon."

Padriag nodded and turned to Maddox Nevin.

"Unlock your weapons, Armiger," Padriag ordered. He keyed the intercom. "All hands, stand by for combat operations."

Maddox was typing quickly.

"All set, sir, whenever you are ready," Maddox said after a moment.

"Helm, full ahead on rotary thrusters and prepare to engage," Padriag ordered. "We'll presumably be coming up behind them and above, so plot several responses, depending on how sharp they are when they look up."

"Aye, sir," Zarah replied.

"Radio, I need exact numbers, locations, and combat estimates, as soon as we clear the horizon," he turned to Nyssa.

"Do we fire a probe up and ahead of us?" she asked.

Padriag considered it.

"Negative, Radio," he decided. "I don't want to give them any warning. Do not even acknowledge that we're coming. This should be a surprise."

"Understood, sir," she said.

Padriag leaned back and drew a breath. Fortunate timing on his part. Or unfortunate. He wasn't sure.

Marrakesh lit the afterburners and started in. On his screen, it almost felt like an atmospheric dogfighter, nosing over and starting a dive, because Zarah had brought them out at a safe distance and relatively low speed, outside the moons and debris fields.

Now, they were charging into harm's way, like an *A'Zedi* warship was supposed to do.

Even a Tactical Transport on what was supposed to be a spy mission.

"Stand by to clear the horizon," Nyssa called after a few minutes. "I'm expecting one medium-sized ship in the middle, plus three or four smaller ones harrying it."

"How are you able to count that?" Padriag asked.

Nyssa looked up at him and blushed.

"Radio waves are bouncing off moons and thermal layers, sir," she said. "Plus, they're all emitting sensor pulses and I've been isolating and trying to identify those."

"Nicely done, Squire," he nodded.

She nodded back and went back to her job.

"Captain, I am fairly certain we will be in range for the heavy particle cannons when we clear," Maddox said. "Do we unmask the Q-Module?"

"Negative, Guns," Padraig replied, somehow hearing the disappointment aft as those folks had to hide a while longer. "Forward battery only, unless they look big enough to waste a missile on."

"Cannon only, aye," he said. "Stand by to engage."

And then *Marrakesh* bounced over the horizon, like a high-speed railcar running away down a slippery slope.

Marrakesh had a pair of heavy twin particle cannon turrets, two barrels in each, one turret on the bow and one on the stern. Additionally, there were regular particle cannons on the four corners. Mostly, those were for defense, but at this range they might be useful to attack as well.

Padraig watched his screen fill with data.

Scrap Transporter Delilah, sitting the middle, four or five times the size of the ships above and behind it. Those four smaller ships weren't identifying themselves with transponders, but Padraig wasn't surprised, if they were pirates. They were firing into *Delilah* but hadn't damaged the ship badly yet.

"Guns, engage," Padraig ordered, just to make it official.

Maddox was already firing.

They'd had regular training on the flight out, dropping out of Ghost-space to pick out some asteroid or rogue moon to blast. Sometimes charging. Sometimes fleeing. More than once blasting by at high speed, just so Maddox and his various gunners got used to different scenarios.

As Captain, Padraig always considered it his primary job to make sure that everyone else on this ship was trained to immediately and competently step up to the next several jobs on their command chain. He understood that other captains didn't feel that way, but they were wrong.

Maddox had lined up his first shot on a spot Nyssa had marked. And she'd hit that one with a bullseye, because they hardly had to lift or slide the big guns to shoot.

"Pirate vessels, this is the *A'Zedi* cruiser *Marrakesh*," Nyssa suddenly cut in on all frequencies. "You will surrender immediately or be destroyed. Strike your colors. You will not get a second warning."

Somebody fired at them. Maddox fired back.

The first pirate ship simply detonated as the beam spiked it at short range.

Pretty, too, because everybody was low enough that Ecix's atmosphere was able to fluoresce various gases with the released energy.

"A-battery, I have a clear shot. Engaging."

"B-battery, first shot missed as target is evading. Might need help to box him in."

"D-battery, no targets in my engagement window. Feel free to overfly at speed. I want a shot at somebody."

"C-battery. Ask somebody else. Bullseye. Target is seriously wounded."

"Main Turret. Target four is dead meat. You folks need any help finishing them off?"

"Negative, Main."

"All turrets, stand down," Nyssa suddenly called. "Repeat, stand down. I have one surrendering and one appears to be damaged sufficiently that they will fall into the atmosphere shortly. Captain, do we wish to rescue them?"

"Have they all surrendered?" Padraig asked.

"Stand by," Nyssa said. "Enemy vessel, this is *Marrakesh*. You are de-orbiting. Do you wish to be rescued, or to die gloriously in battle? Respond on this frequency."

Padraig suppressed a smile. Normally, Nyssa always looked like she was expecting to do something wrong and get yelled at. No doubt leftovers from her home life as a teenager before enlisting.

Then she locked in when trouble started, and a different woman emerged. Cunning. Lethal.

An *A'Zedi* naval officer.

"Captain, they've had enough and request rescue operations," Nyssa turned back to him, calmer now. "Both vessels acknowledge surrender."

Padraig nodded.

"Put me on a general frequency," he ordered, waiting for her to nod. "All vessels, this is Captain Padraig Boru of the *A'Zedi* vessel

Marrakesh. You will place yourself in a safe orbit while we rescue the crew of vessel number three, then stand by to be boarded. Anybody running at this point gets hunted down and destroyed without any mercy. This is not a request. This is a statement of fact. Stand down and stand by."

He nodded to Nyssa, and she cut the line. Padraig dialed a number on his armrest.

"Security. Farrell."

"Farrell, take a full security and medical team with you and board the damaged vessel first," he ordered. "We'll rendezvous with the other one in orbit, then you'll board after dropping your prisoners on *Marrakesh*. Questions?"

"If they resist us, sir?" she asked.

That was what he liked about Cameron Farrell. Tall, muscular woman. Lead Expert E6. Not someone who would take any shit from anyone at any time.

"Get your ass clear because we'll blow their ship to hell and them with it," Padraig replied. "I can always rescue you in free flight."

"Understood, Captain," she said. "My team is in motion."

Padraig cut the line with a nod.

"Captain, I have a Captain Wendell Olafsson on the line to speak with you," Nyssa spoke up. "He's the captain of the ship we rescued, the *Scrap Transporter Delilah*."

Padraig considered it. He looked at the arrangement of ships in orbit as *Marrakesh* backed engines and slowed sharply. *Delilah* was hammered but flying. One pirate moving slowly to a higher orbit. One falling out. Two marked by debris fields slowly cooling and expanding.

"I'll take it in my office," he said. "Chance, you have command."

4

____

Padraig settled in his other favorite chair and drew a breath to let some of the adrenaline wash out of his system. Battles like that always felt like they lasted mere seconds, and at the same time maybe days.

This one had at least been over quickly, once *Marrakesh* surprised the bad guys.

He keyed the line live, noting the chyron across the bottom identifying Wendell Olafsson.

Older man. Dark hair on the sides, bald on top. Lots of freckles. Skinny. Worn face, but smiles now.

"Greetings, Captain Olafsson," Padraig said. "I'm Captain Padraig Boru of the *A'Zedi* Tactical Transport *Marrakesh*. Glad we were close enough to help."

"You have no idea how happy I am to see you, Boru," Olafsson replied. "What brings you to Varfelis?"

"Mostly survey work," Padraig lied facilely, sticking to his cover. "*A'Zedi* would like to send more ships exploring the interior, and this looked like a good truck stop to refuel, but all of our records are sadly out of date."

"You going to invade us?" Olafsson asked sharply.

"Is there even a planet here to invade?" Padraig asked with a laugh. "Last I knew, it was a couple of stations and a variety of ships that come and go. Not even sure how you could hold something like this."

It wasn't like planetary systems were all that valuable, all by themselves. Even this one was no more or less interesting than half a dozen others within ten light-years. Location sort of made it useful, but someone wanting to capture it would end up having to haul in almost everything from somewhere else, and none of the planets in the Iron Zone were habitable to anything except underground mines that weren't likely to be all that profitable.

You can get most minerals from asteroids cheaper. Crops would have to be grown elsewhere.

"Just wondering, *Marrakesh*," Olafsson nodded. "People around here tend to be a bit prickly about outsiders."

"Well, we're hoping to mine some, then trade for credit at the station to help the economy," Padraig smiled to the man's image. "Then meet everyone and make friends. How bad is the piracy problem around here?"

"They caught me off-guard, Boru," Olafsson scowled. "Was hauling supplies out for some of the miners who like to stay here as long as they can to fill their tanks. Might have been a setup. I'd have probably lost my ship and my crew."

"What will the station do with my prisoners?" Padraig asked. "Or will I need to haul them off to an *A'Zedi* world at some point?"

"Not sure, Captain," Olafsson replied. "They weren't folks I knew, so they might be newcomers around here. Varfelis Station is usually neutral ground, so they might fine them and imprison them for a time. Might sell them on a labor contract to work off. You keeping their ships?"

"The one is about to fall into Ecix and be lost," Padraig said. "I don't see a reason to try to salvage it. The other, I haven't made a decision yet."

"You should keep it, then," Olafsson said. "Sell it at the station for even more credit, so you don't have to spent a month sucking gas first."

"That sounds like an excellent idea, Captain," Padraig said. "Thank you. Will you be headed to the station from here?"

"That's the plan, since this run was a bust," the man nodded. "Unless you have need for foodstuffs and spare parts?"

"Food, yes," Padraig replied. "Doubt that your spare parts would be useful for us, unless it's all *A'Zedi* manufacture."

Olafsson laughed.

"Most of it is actually *Wronlori, Marrakesh*," he said. "There have been a lot of those folks come through here lately. You might watch your step."

"Any ships big enough to threaten us?" Padraig asked sharply.

"Oh no, Captain," Olafsson replied. "More likely you'll get swarmed like I did. Bunch more pirates than there used to be. Not sure whether I should pick up stakes and move on somewhere else."

"Well, at least let me buy you a drink at the station, Captain Olafsson," Padraig offered. "We'll be headed that way shortly."

"Looking forward to it, Boru," the man said. "See you there."

And he cut the line.

Padraig leaned back and thought. More piracy than usual. More aggressive, too, from the way the man had spoken. *Wronlori* parts.

Were they in the process of making their own push into this sector? Was that why Gelashvili had sent *Marrakesh*?

There was so much he didn't know. At least he had a sharp crew to find these things out.

5

———

Cameron—Lead Security Expert Farrell—studied the readout as *Flight of Fancy* came alongside the wounded and dying duck, low in Ecix's skies. She turned back to her team and scowled. A dozen faces scowled back behind faceshields.

"Radio Officer Taggart says crew was five," Cameron said. "Weapons will be live until we have cleared the vessel. Medical team, we will either bring them to you, or draw you directly in, but you will remain here until I say otherwise. Questions?"

Nobody had any. They had all trained for this sort of thing, but never actually done it.

Pop quiz time, but Cameron did that enough with her people that they were more bored than nervous.

Exactly what you wanted out of a team of killers about to storm an enemy vessel.

"Farrell, stand by to dock," Rafferty called from forward.

They had the Air Boss flying them today. Flight Deck Chief himself, second only to the Boatswain among the enlisted crew.

Walter just liked to fly any opportunity available.

Cameron moved to the airlock and checked her pistol. She had an Adjustable Disruptor, dialed down to engage at short ranges. Really, a handheld particle cannon that would knock somebody on their ass if they gave her any reason. Couple of folks behind her had heavier

Disruptor Bombardiers, but that was for blasting out locked bulkheads if they had to.

Anybody shooting at her and she'd open the vents and kill every single person on the ship, surrendered once or not.

Flight of Fancy thumped once, then rattled as the airlock hooked itself on.

"Farrell, I read positive pressure on the other side," Rafferty called. "Equalized and ready for you to open the hatch."

She nodded and smacked the button with her offhand, almost smelling the pent-up energy from her people behind her. Even through sealed suits.

The far end of the airlock opened, and she saw a man standing there, hands out where she could see them.

"On your knees," she yelled over the external speakers. "Hands laced on your head. Only warning."

Man didn't feel like being a hero. He dropped, eyes on her. A second person behind him did the same.

Cameron moved to the other end of the airlock behind her disruptor.

"Where are the others?" she demanded.

"Two dead," the first man replied nervously. "Last one's trying to keep us flying."

Cameron nodded. She signaled part of her team to take these two into custody. Another part would hold the airlock. Three followed her deeper.

Nevin, her boss, had nailed this ship pretty solid. Walking down the main corridor aft, she saw the entire port side marked with vacuum warnings, meaning all those cabins had lost seal. From what she'd seen on approach, some of them wouldn't even hold shipping containers, let alone air.

She got to a bulkhead hatch and keyed it. It slid aside, revealing the ass of someone face down inside some piece of equipment.

"*A'Zedi* navy," she yelled. "Time to go."

Turned out to be a woman when she surfaced, but her suit erased all gender until Cameron saw her face.

"Probably just as well," the woman engineer said. "Think it's going to explode anyway. We should get the hell out of here."

Cameron took a look around. Mostly red lights everywhere, a few blinking madly. Haze in the air from wires burning inside walls.

She gestured the woman to precede her, locked on both sides by Cameron's troopers. Quickly, they made their way forward, then crossed out the airlock.

"Rafferty, separate us and back away," Cameron called as she closed up the airlock.

Flight of Fancy rattled some more, then jarred once as he vectored all his thrust up and away from the terminally damaged pirate.

"What the hell are you people doing here, anyway?" the woman engineer asked, surrounded and sitting.

"There's a new sheriff in town," Cameron smiled at her.

6

———

Chance Messier hadn't commanded something like this since she was a pup, so she was kinda enjoying herself. Small vessel. Mostly an armed freighter designed to be as automated as possible. Captain forward. Three other seats, with one beside her and two on her flanks, facing sideways and able to turn forward.

From the factory, it probably required only one crew member, but more recent owners had done things to it, to the point that she was happy to have an engineer aft watching the extra systems that had been bolted and welded in wherever there was space. Chance didn't figure she'd need the top-mounted turret manned, nor a space gunner forward next to her, but Cameron had insisted on her carrying a full crew.

Chance opened a line back to *Marrakesh*.

"*A'Zedi* armed transport *Tyrannosaurus* to *Marrakesh*," she said, smiling, even as Cameron rolled her eyes.

"Very funny," Padraig replied. "Go ahead."

"We've completed a quick inspection and are ready to follow you to the station whenever you give the word."

"Excellent news, Chance," he said. "Stand by."

Zarah Halloran came on the line next. Piloting.

"*Tyrannosaurus*, *Marrakesh* will transition to Ghostdrives in five, four, three, two, one..."

And they were gone.

Chance had been rocking her head to the beat and bounced up and out immediately after, to the point that both ships showed up on the Aetherial boards as a single dot.

Everyone was traveling slow, since this was a long in-system hop, but it still only took less than thirty seconds before they dropped out again.

Innermost gas giant, known to the locals apparently as Sybeth. Big monster. Small brown dwarf that gave off more heat than it absorbed, though it would never have enough mass to trigger fusion and become a full star.

Golds and reds dominated the bands of clouds going back and forth below them. Pretty. Mess of moons moving around, plus her scanners showed dozens of ships nearby, with dozens more docked to the station itself.

Varfelis Station was a barbell shape, bulbed at both ends, with a small ring around the center like a belt.

"Weird looking," Cameron offered as they started their approach.

"Refineries at both ends," Chance said, digging back deep into her desk jockey days, when she'd almost taken a station assignment, just to get off the surface. "I'm guessing that ships dock at the top as we're looking in order to disgorge all the gases that they mine from various giants around here. Those get sorted, cracked, refined, and stored at the bottom end, then you can either dock there to refuel yourself, or a big transport will load up and haul it all off to some factory somewhere. Small one, considering the number of gas and ice giants in the system, so either they're efficient at what they do, or they've never been able to upgrade."

"Piracy suggests the latter," Cameron offered.

"It does," Chance agreed. "And a place like this might not be able to hire a squadron or warship big enough to drive them off."

"Is that why we're here?" Cam asked.

Chance looked over and studied the woman. Security Lead, but not an officer. Excellent at close combat, but Padraig had instructed her to keep the ship's new mission somewhat under wraps. At least for as long as possible. That included lies and evasions to the crew.

For now, anyway.

"We're here because fleet wants to know if this would make a useful truck stop," Chance replied carefully. "If they knew we were coming and had a lot of tankers lined up and ready to refill things as quickly as we might empty them, they might be. For now, no fleet can take advantage of this, but cruisers and scouts can. That much we've learned. There's more."

Cameron nodded and shut up. Smart woman who didn't want to become an officer, because then she couldn't be in charge of security teams storming captured pirates or enemy warships.

And Chance knew what Cam really wanted.

They shared a smile.

"*A'Zedi* transport *Tyrannosaurus*, this is Varfelis Station," a new, male voice came on the line. "Docking instructions transmitted. We understand that your ship is a captured and reflagged pirate vessel?"

"That is correct, Station Command," Chance replied. "We rescued *Scrap Transport Delilah* at Ecix and captured one of the four vessels attacking them. *Marrakesh* is transporting prisoners for you. I have only a prize crew aboard."

There was a pause as he digested that. Varfelis was way far away from the wars of the rims. *A'Zedi* and *Wronlori* ships would call, but this was probably the first time an *A'Zedi* warship had been seen in this system in years.

"Understood, *Tyrannosaurus*," he finally said. "We'll have a customs officer meet you at the gate, but it sounds like we need to dock *Marrakesh* for the important details."

"Correct, Station Command," Chance said. "See you shortly."

She cut the line and reviewed the docking instructions, keying them manually into the autopilot. This little ship had flown just fine when they were testing it. And the jaunt over had been smooth enough that she was willing to trust that the pirates had been maintaining it.

Padraig would be delivering them to justice shortly.

What she didn't know was what justice looked like at a place like Varfelis Station.

7

———

Padraig sized up his prisoners. Seven of them, out of supposedly nineteen across four hulls. All were handcuffed but hadn't given him any trouble.

Even now, the shock of their capture was still slow to wear off, so they were moving like badly programmed automatons. Having a large force of armed sailors around them did help immensely with their manners.

Marrakesh barely dinged as she backed into the docking bay and connected.

"Stand by for airlock deployment," Zarah called over the intercom.

Padraig nodded and waited. Mostly hisses and thumps, then the airlock hatch began to beep and open. Cameron Farrell was with Chance, but he had Trinh Hoàng, Security Expert E5. Tiny woman, so today she had slung her Light Disruptor Cannon over her shoulder, mostly as a statement of purpose, since it was almost as long as she was tall.

That helped with keeping pirates polite, too.

The hatch opened and he followed Trinh into the corridor, emerging on the far side to a small mob. About half felt like pedestrians watching a traffic accident, being held back by a few security troops and a line of waist-high barricades. On this side of the barricade, two figures stood out, amidst more security folks in their gray uniforms.

The woman was average in size, with a fairish complexion of the sort Padraig usually associated with *Wronlori*. She was dressed in a nicer business suit.

The man next to her was dressed in the same gray uniform as the security troopers in view. He was, however, a giant. Two hundred and ten centimeters tall. Maybe most of that wide, at least at the shoulders. Skin so dark that it might actually be black, and one of the few folks Padraig had seen who was darker than the average *A'Zedi* citizen.

Padraig felt like a child as he stepped close.

"Captain Boru?" she asked, holding out a hand to shake.

"That's right," he said, taking it.

"I am Diana Mendoza, Mayor of Varfelis Station," she nodded. "This is Emmett Martinez, Chief of Police."

Padraig shook the man's hand. It was like holding hands with a bear.

"Chief," he said simply, smiling up at the scowling man.

"Understand from Wendell Olafsson that you have prisoners for me?" Martinez growled in a voice that sounded like someone had roused him mid-winter.

"We do," Padraig nodded. "I wasn't sure what protocols were appropriate here, so I have them ready to hand over, if you're ready to take charge of them."

He nodded to Trinh, and she pulled up a handcom.

"Bring them out," she ordered. "Got locals here for them."

Padraig shifted around and watched as his people marched out the pirates, handing them over to Chief Martinez. Quickly, the Chief's folks got them gone, but the Chief himself remained.

Padraig nodded his thanks to the man and turned back to the mayor.

Mayor? What an interesting title. Especially on a space station.

"Wendell speaks highly of you," she said with a compact, wry smile. "As one might expect, having just been rescued. He also said that you were scouting?"

"*A'Zedi* would like to send exploration missions deeper into the galactic interior," Padraig answered, sticking to his cover story. "They tasked *Marrakesh* with exploring Varfelis and a few other systems, to see if any of them could make useful staging and refueling stops for those ships."

After all, someone trying to use Varfelis to attack a *Wronlori* world would still have a long sail, even if it did let them sneak all the way around the back. Same as it would let a *Wronlori* squadron.

"I see," Mayor Mendoza said noncommittally. "And the captured ship called *Tyrannosaurus*?"

"Wendell Olafsson suggested that I might be able to sell it locally for a good chunk of credit," Padraig replied. "We had expected originally to simply call on the station as a quick courtesy, before moving off and spending a few weeks mining gases for things we could sell here, before loading up to haul refined products back to our base."

He waited. Gelashvili had worked it all out, but she had also warned him that they would be operating a great distance from home, in a place where friendly warships wouldn't be able to quickly come to their rescue if they got into trouble.

Marrakesh was on their own, but he honestly had the best damned crew in the fleet backing him up.

She looked up at the tall Chief, looming over everyone in here. That man nodded. Padraig wasn't sure what communication passed, but it didn't feel like trouble.

And he had Trinh standing slightly off to one side. Martinez might be big, but Trinh was mean when she wanted to be. And expecting trouble, from the slight smile on her face.

Maybe Martinez saw that, too.

Mendoza looked around at the quiet mob watching her back.

"The party is over," she announced in that Mom voice that got people moving unconsciously. "Go back to whatever you were doing."

Folks started to edge away. Padraig grinned when she turned back to him.

"You have certainly brought a bit of excitement, Captain Boru," she opined. "Let's go back to my office and see about filling out paperwork."

Padraig nodded.

So far, so good.

8

Kaitlin smiled as she transited onto the station and turned right. Walked like a tourist, dressed in civilian clothes.

She was still getting used to the job of Ship's Stevedore, even after a year and change. For her entire career, she'd been an enlisted punk, rising after thirty years to the rank of Docker, the enlisted position Den Gilroy held now just below her, with her in charge.

And, she supposed, she could have sent Den, but that would have taken away all her fun, so Kaitlin had gone aboard the station herself. Technically, she and Chance Messier were supposed to split the duties of resupply, but they'd worked so well together that Chance just nodded and smiled most of the time. Plus, Chance was off selling a slightly-used pirate ship.

So Kaitlin got to handle resupply.

It both helped and hindered that *Marrakesh* had been sent out here on a spy mission, according to Padraig. They had the Q-Module, which was all guns and missiles when it should have been cargo, so they'd taken to filling every spare room and half-abandoned corridor on the ship with boxes of supplies so that they could pretend to outsiders like they had that cargo space. The Gas Module wasn't much help there, either, as it was an extremely small refinery and a whole series of massive tanks that could be filled by lowering hoses into the atmosphere of a gas giant.

Marrakesh simply didn't have the space that they might have had, with any two other modules.

Today, she had to handle resupply a little sideways. Keep things simple and fill up more frequently than she would have liked to.

At the same time, she didn't have to do much today, as they were still emptying boxes and freeing up space.

The flight home, that would be a different beast. She'd deal with it later.

Varfelis Station struck her for grunginess as she walked. Lots of lights, all pouring pure white illumination down in a way that almost made it worse than if some were out.

They needed a more yellow hue. More like firelight. Warmer and inviting. That was it. Varfelis Station was cold, in spite of the temperature being perfectly normal.

Emotionally aloof. Not a lot of plants, when most stations she'd visited had pots in every corner and atop every filing cabinet, both for the oxygen-generating effect and the ability to bear fruit.

Or at least make things more homey.

Long corridor, curving away to her left as it circled the station's waist. Docking bays and airlocks on the outer edge. Small shops and offices on the right. Mix of mom-and-pop places, about even with galactic chains.

Kaitlin wondered how expensive it was to ship food and dry goods all the way out here. Probably just sent a massive container ship every six months or so, then left containers either docked or hanging nearby in space until needed.

Wasn't like everything wasn't trucked in here from somewhere else. Even the hydroponics she had heard about wouldn't do much more than feed the rich folks fresh salad.

She found her hatch, pushing the button to open it and sliding in.

A woman sat behind the desk, confused apparently when she didn't recognize Kaitlin.

Kaitlin got it. Small station, out in the middle of nowhere. Probably pretty insular.

"May I help you?" the woman asked hesitantly.

"Kaitlin Lynch," she introduced herself. "Stevedore off of *Marrakesh*. Station Control said that this was the place to talk to about our resupply."

"*Marrakesh*?" the woman gasped. "Well, yes, please sit down. What can I help you with?"

Kaitlin grinned and took the seat.

Small office. Cluttered. Homey after the sterility of the corridor. Couple of plants, which was a good sign. Older woman, a little worn and tired looking. Maybe Kaitlin's age, but she never felt fifty-three. Too young at heart, making the kids look bad by comparison.

But it was a starting point. An entry point into this system. Padraig needed several of those.

"Well, we've brought some trade goods with us," Kaitlin began. "And we'll be selling a captured pirate ship once we talk to a few people. Past that, I needed to talk to someone about the sorts of things that we might purchase, versus those things that don't really exist here. We're strangers and nobody knew what to expect."

"I'm Adrian Sanchez, Ms. Lynch," the woman nodded, pulling a reader from the piles of paper in front of her. "Let's just see where we are."

Kaitlin leaned back and smiled as the woman started asking questions.

At least they were better prepared than a normal transport pulling into dock.

9

———

Chance had docked *Tyrannosaurus* and shut everything down. She had Cam and a small team with her, waiting until Padraig sorted out the station.

Hell of a way to say hello, showing up and capturing a pirate ship. And blowing up three others.

Then someone rang the door buzzer, down in the airlock.

Chance found herself staring at Cam, only to get a shrug back.

"Station should have said something, if they were sending someone," Chance noted.

Cam was up out of her seat with a pistol in hand so fast Chance nearly missed her heading aft. She followed the woman at a safe distance.

"Security to the airlock," Cam yelled.

Quickly, two more crew members joined her. Chance stayed back, standing in the hatch to the small cargo hold where she could duck back and trigger the bulkhead if she had to.

Cameron looked around, placing her two crew members mostly out of sight behind a couple of boxes Chance had inherited with the ship. Space parts and meal packs, for the most part. Poverty of the sort that caused people to turn to piracy.

Hopefully, nobody was intending to take the ship back, right here on the concourse.

Cameron nodded to herself, opened the airlock, and pointed her pistol out of sight from what Chance could see.

A male voice rumbled, but the words were indistinct.

"Negative," Cameron replied. "Security Lead Farrell. In command of the boarding party."

More rumbles. Definitely male. One voice. Cam wasn't nervous.

She did glance over.

"Man here wants to talk to you about the ship, Commander," Cam said, eyes and pistol still aimed at the man, presumably.

"Is he armed?" Chance asked.

"Not visibly," Cam replied. "He'll get frisked before he boards, though."

The man said something.

"Step into the airlock, then," Cam ordered. "I'll close the far end. Put your hands on the sidewall and spread your feet."

The pistol never wavered, until Cam holstered it with a nod to her troopers. She vanished into the airlock.

Ten seconds passed.

A tall, heavy-set white man emerged. Pale. Almost albino pink. Definitely *Wronlori* stock originally, however far from home he was.

Weren't they all?

"Commander Messier, this is Abraham Ferrari," Cam said. "Wants to talk to you."

Chance stepped deeper into the cargo hold and sized the man up. Extremely tall. At least one hundred and ninety centimeters, but pear shaped around the middle and soft in ways that you didn't see in the navy.

Only civilians, where they didn't have quarterly fitness reports.

He was dressed in slacks and loose-fitting burnous over a tunic, all done in shades of tan. His hood was back, and he had a short cylindrical peakless hat, done in deep red, that she thought was called a fez, but would have to look that term up.

Chance didn't get too close, but close enough that she wasn't yelling at the man.

"Mister Ferrari?" she asked, being polite.

"Commander Messier," he bowed deeply, smiling in an oily kind of way that made her want to take a shower when he was gone. "I'm given to understand from the rumor mill that your ship captured this vessel and is in the process of perhaps putting it up for sale?"

Chance found herself getting a headache, just trying to parse his syntax. Still, his intent was clear enough.

"That is correct, sir," she offered. "At present, my captain is working with the station authorities to establish the correct process, so perhaps you would be best suited talking to them."

"Indeed, Commander," he nodded. "Indeed, indeed. However, I wished to, if you will allow me a bit of coloring outside the lines, to examine the ship in its current state, that I might determine if I wished to bid on the matter when it moved forward. As you know, sometimes things like this are handled quietly and without the sorts of delay and fuss that would accompany a public auction."

Chance found his colorful language to at least be charming enough, for all the man was a fast-talker. A used camel salesman, as some of her friends might have described the man.

"I cannot speak to that, Mister Ferrari," Chance smiled. "How does the station normally handle confiscated goods?"

He paused, as if taken back by her words.

"Madam, it is highly unusual that such a thing even happens at Varfelis Station," he finally said crisply. "Piracy, having previously been practically unknown, has suddenly moved to the stage of nearly endemic. My own ships are at risk every time they move beyond the safety zone this station enforces upon its surroundings by means of superior firepower. Being able to protect themselves against marauders such as you have already battered is a great value to the system, and to myself, were I able to take advantage of the situation."

Chance smiled and shrugged, unwilling to be drawn deeper into conversation with the man. She wasn't entirely sure what he might offer her if she gave him an inch.

"It flies well, Mister Ferrari," she offered instead. "I'm certain that Captain Boru will undertake to have an inspector come aboard and report her findings. Until such time, however, I feel that it would perhaps be unfair to your competitors to let you have that much of an advantage when it came to bidding, so I must ask you to depart now. You can route your questions to *Marrakesh* after this."

He smiled and started to say something, but Cam growled at the man, and he blinked in surprise.

"Boss asked you to depart," Cam said firmly. "Are you walking or being tossed out on your ass?"

Again, he opened his mouth as if to say something effusive but closed it when he realized that Cam would be happy to knock him down and drag him the length of the airlock. And had two helpers who were also smiling.

"Good day, indeed, ladies," he said quickly. "I shall see myself out and look forward to dealing with you again in the future."

Chance smiled and let Cam chase him out.

"What the hell was that all about?" Cameron asked when she returned a few moments later.

"Beats me," Chance said. "However, I need to warn Padraig, I think, that the man's heading his way."

The others chuckled.

They sure as hell had made a splash around here.

Was it a good one?

10

───────

Nyssa was still getting used to her fabulous new toys. And a whole subset of functions, already built into the datacore, that were normally well beyond her rank and responsibilities, even as primary Radio Officer on *Marrakesh*.

Spy shit.

However, she'd earned her latest set of stripes at Monsanch, cracking a *Wronlori* diplomatic code. Granted, not a particularly complicated one, as they went, but good enough that she'd spent two weeks reading messages as fast as they could be decrypted.

Here, as at Monsanch, they were the only warship in scan range. The only vessel not entirely civilian, as far as she could tell, but Nyssa had learned not to take anything at face value.

Especially not after she'd been quietly taken aside to be told and shown some things that not even the captain was privy to. She was, on her discretion, allowed to tell him, but hadn't as yet.

She might be a little power mad with it all, but at least she was willing to admit it.

Maddox Nevin had command. Captain, Commander Messier, and even the Stevedore were off-ship right now, which was highly unusual. But so was the situation.

Nyssa was at her station, with extra things available that only unlocked when she added a second password.

Power.

First rule of electronic espionage: Don't break anything. Find ways in, then plant bugs and avatars that could listen, but didn't make any changes that might compromise your access.

Varfelis Station was a small city in the middle of nowhere, and everyone on the station had to work with the authorities at all times. Power, water, sewage. Everything came from a central system that was protected about as well as the average corporate entity back home.

Sledgehammering the access points with ten million password attempts would probably get someone's attention, so she settled for accessing the library system. And uploading the last five years' worth of daily newspapers from Horwin back home, brought along exactly for this purpose.

The Aetherial communications array was great for sending messages at ultra-fast FTL, but they tended to be expensive, so not a lot of data was transmitted. And you sure as hell didn't broadcast general news on one, so gossip and box scores only moved as fast as ships carrying them.

So, they got the "Horwin Herald." Five years' worth from the *A'Zedi* capital. Somebody would appreciate that.

Next, she dialed in to let folks on the ship request books from the local public library, after sending them through all manner of defensive scans to keep out folks trying to do to her what she was doing to the station.

Information Security. *Infosec* at the highest level.

Later, she would try a few things, but they were mostly here to scout, not to set the place up for an invasion.

At least according to what she'd been told. Anything was possible.

"Radio," Maddox called to get her attention. "What's the immediate vicinity like?"

She was also in charge of sensors, so she quick-scanned that data and sent it on.

"Main station where we're docked," she replied. "Almost a score of other, smaller stations nearby, about half of which appear to be old ships placed in a contemporary orbit but not capable of free flight. Mostly storage, it looks like, where you can bring something from somewhere else, and it's cheaper to put it there than on the main.

About fifty ships, either docked or close by. Seven larger than us by tonnage, but nothing armed to our scale."

"How well armed are these vessels?" Maddox asked.

Nyssa paused and reviewed some of her passive observations. Then compared them with the four ships *Marrakesh* had killed or captured at Ecix.

"Everyone appears armed, sir," she replied. "Literally everyone. And pretty heavily, too. Lots of what we might classify as light particle cannon as well as standard. Good for short range, either offense or defense. Most look welded on instead of designed that way, if that makes sense?"

She looked up and he nodded.

"Sir?" she asked.

"Welded on, Squire," he said firmly, sounding a lot like the captain, which was a compliment. "After they came from the factory. It means that they didn't used to need particle cannons to protect themselves. The key will be figuring out how long ago something changed. I doubt you'll be able to determine that, but useful if you come across something."

Nyssa nodded, then thought back to the newspapers she had delivered. The everyday gossip that could be culled for larger trends.

Could she do the same here?

"You had a thought?" Maddox asked.

"Maybe, sir," she nodded. "We have access to their public library. That might have newspapers and things we can scan through. Is it important?"

"Low to medium, Taggart," he replied. "Might help the Captain understand things better, but not worth dropping everything else to determine. That make sense?"

"It does, sir," she said. "I will add it to the list."

He nodded and went back to his boards. Nyssa considered how she might scientifically identify those trends. Keywords, coalesced into date ranges? In her spare time, she'd started studying some arcane and highly advanced mathematics, mostly to understand what some of her tools could do.

Data needed to be turned into information, but aggregating it only got you so far. You had to understand confidence levels and reliability.

But yeah, she might be able to do some things.

And if piracy was a growing problem around here, did that make things better or worse?

11

—————

Captain Alex Carson didn't like it. Not one damned bit. And there wasn't anything he could do about it, either.

He turned to his Jeremy, his First Mate.

"Jeremy, what can we do against an *A'Zedi* cruiser?" Alex asked.

"Hard question, Alex," Jeremy replied. "On the one hand, it's not a full cruiser, but a tug hauling pods. On the other hand, it's still damned big. Looks like they are more heavily armed than any police frigate we might have run into."

"Have we scanned *Marrakesh* yet?" Alex asked, looking around his bridge.

He liked to keep the space a little dark. Gloomy, perhaps. Imposing and intimidating, as befit a ship like *Hellhound*. Same with the paint. Darker gray instead of pretty colors fops and fools used to brighten their lives.

Captain Alex Carson would have painted things the color of dried blood, but figured that might be one step too far, even for his crew of cutthroats.

Jeremy Luna was off to one side. Mostly, his First Mate handled scanners and targeting systems, while Alex controlled the offense. They made a pretty good team.

Jeremy shrugged and grimaced, all at once.

"Beyond the basic sort of thing you do when a ship gets close, no,"

Jeremy said. "didn't think we wanted the attention focused on us, ya know?"

Alex bit back a snarl. The man was right.

"Set up a pattern for optical observation," Alex ordered. "How many turrets can they deploy? How many missile tubes can we count? That sort of shit. If they're going to be here for a while, we might have a problem. On the other hand, maybe we can go get some friends and overwhelm them. *A'Zedi* is a long ways from here, so it ain't like anyone can help."

Jeremy nodded, face still uncertain.

"What?" Alex demanded.

"We getting paid enough for this?" he asked. "I realize that the money is pretty good, but still…"

It was Alex's turn to nod. *Wronlori* was paying them under the table. Mostly to soften the place up, presumably for a future invasion, though Alex couldn't imagine what the hell they might want with Varfelis as a system. Nothing but gas and ore to mine. Not on a road to anywhere.

"The money is good enough," Alex said, pausing to look around at the half-dozen other crew members in sight. "Remember, our goal is to own this place eventually. Maybe this pushes our date up, maybe it pushes it out. One cruiser won't be worth shit against a swarm, if it comes to that."

Heads nodded, but nobody challenged him. That was good. Captain Alex Carson was in charge around here, and they better remember it.

He turned back to Jeremy.

"Get me an inventory of everyone that we might be able to hire when we go after *Marrakesh*," he ordered. "Snubfighters up to gunboats. If we have to, we'll hire a second carrier to haul folks around, but *A'Zedi* doesn't get to waltz in here and smile. We clear?"

More nods.

Alex rose and stretched.

"Jeremy, you're in charge," he said. "I'm going to get some food and do paperwork. Then we'll figure out how to kill an *A'Zedi* cruiser so we can take over this place for good. Paste that onto your mirrors so you see it every morning. We're going to be in charge of this system.

Nobody else. Even *Wronlori* won't do more than send a couple of ships out to look good. We'll be the power in this system."

He turned and stomped in the direction of the hatch. Food. Then the paperwork beast that never died.

And one interloper he needed to scout, so he could finally take over around here.

12

Padraig rubbed the bridge of his nose and looked at Kaitlin and Chance. His hatch was closed, and his office private.

"So, this Ferrari chap was wanting to inspect the ship, prior to maybe making an offer?" he asked.

"That was my impression, Padraig," Chance nodded. "Also, not a lot of armed ships on the market, so maybe he could lowball us for price, compared to what it was worth?"

"And he might be somebody we wanted to bribe by letting him," Padraig agreed. "We'll need to dig into the local rumor mill and figure out if he's a hero or a villain around here."

"Probably both," Kaitlin spoke up. "Folks like that are usually gray that way. Businessmen, forever hustling against some number in their head. Or maybe against death itself, since the lucky ones don't actually need the money."

"How are we for supplies?" he asked her.

"Good," Kaitlin nodded. "I swapped the station a list of what we carried in terms of excess, for the sorts of things they wanted. All manner of gases can be mined off the various planets. Ores and ice come from asteroids and comets floating around, so nothing in the way of raw materials is all that rare. If somebody sailed a greenhouse ship out here, they probably have a license to print credits, because food mostly has to come from somewhere else, and there aren't any farm colonies all that close."

Padraig turned to Chance.

"Have Zarah and her staff start looking at astrogation records," he ordered. "See if there are worlds around here that might be in a position to swap food for industrial inputs. Maybe someplace on the verge of light manufacturing. If we could set up a trade link to a friendly world, that makes Varfelis look better. And potentially earns us social credit with the locals. What can *Marrakesh* do over the short term to generate income for this system?"

"Gases," Kaitlin replied definitively. "We've got brand new equipment in better shape than most folks around here. And more power, so we ought to be able to dive pretty deep into some of these atmospheres. Maybe deeper than most folks, so we might get better concentrations of things than anybody else. Or new things."

"And you have a list?" he asked.

"Do," Kaitlin nodded. "The third gas giant, Alanta, is the outermost one. Outside that are a pair of ice giants with radically different chemistry. Alanta doesn't get a lot of attention and has a few things we could gather up."

"You and your team let Zarah know and have her start plotting orbital insertions," Padraig ordered. "I figure we've got a week on station, moving some cargo around and selling a small warship. Let's use that to gather as much intelligence as we can."

"Do we host local captains and officials for a cocktail party while we're here?" Chance asked.

Padraig felt his face screw into something a quizzical dog might have shown. Chance grinned at his confusion.

"Rent a space on the station since we don't want folks coming aboard and seeing how cramped we are," she replied. "That might tell them too much. But take some of the credits we're earning and throw a small party to say hello to folks. If nothing else, it lets us divide them into friendly and unfriendly groups pretty quickly."

Padraig considered it. Not his usual thing, but he could see where it might help break the ice around here.

"Let me talk to Nyssa," he said. "She's digging in locally. Maybe we ask Ferrari to host something for us, since he's a gladhander according to Chance?"

"No, let's do it ourselves," Chance countered. "He probably has enemies and rivals that wouldn't come. We want to know who they are as well."

"Okay," he nodded. "Let's figure out what we can sell a pirate vessel for, and what we can do with the credit. Kaitlin, you look into the price and availability to rent us a space and fill it with catering for a party, but don't commit to anything just yet. Chance, you work to make sure we understand everyone flying around."

"We looking for anything in particular?" Chance asked.

"Ferrari said they were all armed," he nodded. "How armed? Maddox mentioned that he had Nyssa looking, so pull all that together. We're not as heavily armed as a line cruiser, at least on paper, so I want to know who might be a threat to us, either as we appear, or as we will be when we blow the panels and open fire with everything else. Someone, somewhere, is pissed at us for blowing up three of his ships and capturing the fourth, along with crews. I don't want him coming after us with more firepower than we can resist. If that means running like hell, then we're back to that damned Leviathan and I need contingency plans for that as well. Questions?"

"Not until I dig deeper," Chance replied.

Kaitlin shook her head. Both rose and left him alone.

Padraig considered how weird things had already gone. He keyed a number.

"Radio, Taggart."

"Nyssa, turn everything over to someone and join me in my office," he ordered. "I have some questions."

13

Nyssa squared her shoulders and entered the day office. Commander Messier and the Stevedore had just left, so something important had been discussed. And she and the captain had their own conspiracy these days.

He was behind his desk. She took the spot on the right in front. It was still warm from somebody's butt. He closed the hatch behind her.

Captain Boru smiled at her. Nyssa waited.

"We're likely to remain either docked to the station or close by for a week," he began. "Considering your other activities, does either impact you more or less?"

Nyssa considered it.

"Docked, I get to connect directly to their systems, sir," she replied. "I've started inserting avatars and things, and I don't think anyone has noticed as yet. If we back off to radio range, all that traffic gets broadcast and someone might listen. Doubt that they could crack it, but just the amount of traffic might tell them more than we want to."

She paused and watched. Captain Boru was young for such a rank and a command, barely fifteen years older than her. At the same time, she'd seen and heard enough, both on the ship and from her new skip boss in Madam Gelashvili, to understand how smart he was. How sharp.

They'd all gotten lucky in being assigned to *Marrakesh*. Captain Boru made his own luck, sometimes.

"In that case, I'll lean towards remaining docked for now," he nodded. "How are you coming on your various research tasks?"

Nyssa felt her face screw sideways as she considered it.

"Piracy started to ramp up about three years ago, sir," she said. "Quietly, like someone boiling a frog, but I was able to start looking at police reports and that trend line starts upwards thirty-four months ago. More arrests for smuggling. More reports of attacks and hijackings. Slowly, but steady. What happened to *Delilah* was one of the most brazen, but only because the bad guys didn't succeed, and instead got crushed when we happened to be close by to help."

He nodded, eyes looking over her right shoulder at something that probably wasn't within a thousand light-years.

"Those four ships," he finally said. "How big of a dent did we make in local piracy circles?"

Nyssa paused before replying, trying to remember her various formulae and results.

"Some, but not a lot," she said. "The pirates always seem to hit from somewhere else, rather than being local vessels."

"Outsiders?" he asked sharply.

"Yes, sir," she nodded. "None of them showed up on local records as having docked at Varfelis Station in the last year when I ran those logs."

"Where did they come from?" he asked. "I'd assumed that we'd run into one of two or three street gangs around here, rumbling with each other. Is there some other system or base nearby that is some sort of pirate den?"

"I don't know, Captain," she replied honestly. She was new at all this, and still making it up as she went. "Would that data be in the ship we captured?"

"You will take a security team aboard that vessel immediately and find out, Squire," he ordered her. "Pack an overnight bag with food and such, in case you need to stay aboard the ship for a few days. Right now, we have a couple of folks aboard, mostly as guards. You need to be prepared to defend the vessel against attack from the station. Am I clear?"

"Aye, sir," she said. "Who should I take?"

She watched him key a number on his pad.

"Security. Farrell."

"Cameron, I want you and Trinh Hoàng to meet Squire Taggart at the aft airlock immediately," he said. "Take a small team that will reside aboard *Tyrannosaurus* until otherwise ordered. Take food, clothing, and armaments sufficient for a detached mission in hostile territory. Questions?"

"None immediately, sir," Cam replied. "We'll be ready in four minutes."

"Excellent, Farrell," he said, cutting the line.

"Would they have deleted the data, sir?" she asked. "Assuming they were smart enough?"

"They can try," he smiled cruelly at her. "But they didn't wipe the whole datacore in the time they had, so all that information is probably still in there somewhere. I need you to find it, because that might be the sort of thing that we send home and call for a squadron to help. Piracy is always bad for business, Squire. It is a breakdown of civilization, and is both caustic and toxic over any long stretch. Even when they aren't subject to *A'Zedi* law, we can still enforce that. I need you telling me where to sail to. Go."

Nyssa considered that and rose, already making a list in her head of things she needed immediately, versus things she could ask the captain to send over later, once she settled. Commander Messier had said that the ship was pretty clean, as far as that went, so she could trust the basics. And there was some food, but nothing anybody would trust.

Mostly, a portable computer with some of her special tools already installed, and maybe someone from Engineering, with all their tools, in case she needed to take apart their datacore and haul pieces back to *Marrakesh*.

She nodded sharply and exited.

Things were getting serious.

14

Padraig leaned back as the hatch closed. He'd lit the right kind of fire under Nyssa's ass. And taking heavy firepower with her would ensure that *Tyrannosaurus* was safe. And maybe he wasn't going to end up selling the ship as quickly as he'd thought, because it might contain evidence of a far wider range of crimes than he'd considered even ten minutes ago.

Varfelis Station security was limited to the sphere that their guns could command, when you got right down to it. And Padraig doubted that there would be any sort of secret base in-system. Too easy to be seen, if someone had the patience.

No, it would be somewhere else, but still close. Perhaps central to a half-dozen places like Varfelis. It was the most important system around here, but not the only one. Just the biggest, in terms of giants that could be mined for useful gases.

He rose and moved to the hatch, studying the bridge when it opened. Nobody immediately reacted, which was good. He wanted his crew focused more on their jobs than on jumping up and saluting when he entered a room, unlike some officers.

Glen Tameron was sitting at Nyssa's station, handling Radio duties right now. Padraig walked up beside him. As dark as most of *A'Zedi*, with hair that probably should have gone to the barber a few days ago, but Tameron was a sharp crew member, and Padraig didn't feel like cracking the whip on anybody today. Morale was exceptional right now.

The man nodded and kept monitoring his screens.

Marrakesh docked meant that they really only saw a slice of space about one hundred and fifty degrees wide, centered on the bow.

"I need to send a message to Wendell Olafsson," Padraig said. "Captain of *Scrap Transporter Delilah*. Are we connected with the station well enough to handle it?"

"Aye, sir," Tameron replied. "We've got a number where we can ping, or a message box, depending on your needs."

"Drop a message in his box and ask him to call me here when he has an opportunity," Padraig ordered. "Then roust me from whatever I might be doing, including sleeping, when he does. Clear?"

"Aye, sir," Tameron said. "Connect him inbound at any time, sir."

Padraig nodded and headed back to his office. There was a chance that Olafsson would call immediately, so he might as well spend a half hour handy, just in case. After that, he'd do some inspections.

Padraig settled in his chair, back in his office, as a light blinked. He brought the line live.

"Captain Olafsson for you, sir," Tameron said immediately.

"Put him through," Padraig said. "Video available?"

"Aye, sir," Tameron replied. "Video coming up."

Padraig pushed the button to bring his vid screen live on the far wall. Wendell Olafsson was there immediately, smiling.

Padraig hadn't really paid that close of attention to the man before. Perhaps fifty, tall and skinny with dark hair and pale skin.

"Captain Boru," Olafsson smiled. "How can I be of assistance this afternoon?"

"I had a couple of questions about piracy, Captain Olafsson," Padraig replied. "And thought I might invite you aboard for a meal and a conversation, where we could talk at length."

He didn't mention the part about not being overheard in the process. If they were aboard *Marrakesh*, Padraig could control things, at least until Olafsson decided to gossip later. At the same time, anything that came out of those conversations could be traced back to Olafsson easily enough, if they were true.

Or marked up to bullshit rumors if they weren't.

"That would be lovely, Captain," Olafsson replied. "I'm not really much of an expert on the topic, though. You might be better off talking to Mayor Mendoza or Chief Martinez."

"I'm certain of that," Padraig replied. "And I'll chat with them at some point. I've had some things come up recently that don't fit in with the rest of the puzzle, though, and hoped that a fresh perspective might be useful. And I have a pretty good cook in my wardroom."

Olafsson considered it, from the look on his face. Concern. Avarice. Confusion. Whatever.

"Okay," he finally said. "Not sure what I know, but happy to answer questions. If nothing else, I can point you at folks who might know better."

"And that is exactly why I wanted to chat, Olafsson," Padraig nodded. "We don't really know folks around here, so I don't even know who to talk to."

"Oh, I can help there," the man said, relieved. "When's good to come aboard?"

"I'll go to dinner in about four hours," Padraig replied. "Then breakfast in about twelve after that. What works on your schedule?"

"I could be ready to come aboard in four hours," the man said.

"Excellent," Padraig said. "I'll see you then."

The man nodded and Padraig cut the line, then dialed a different one.

"Wardroom. Quirke."

"This is Captain Boru," Padraig said. "I'll have a civilian guest joining me for dinner in four hours, if you wanted to do something to impress him, Chief."

"Gotcha, Cap," the man replied. Padraig could hear the sudden excitement in his voice. "We'll have something special for you."

"Thank you," and he cut the line.

Padraig rested his chin on his hands and wondered what they had stumbled into here.

15

———

Nyssa was a little nervous to be leading a small army, but Captain had been quite clear. And taking this deadly serious.

Folks on the concourse stopped what they were doing and watched Nyssa and her mob in mulberry and mauve trooping along. Her heavily armed mob leading two big trunks on rollers.

At one point, a local security officer emerged from a shop, talking into a handheld radio as he watched them. Nyssa smiled at the man and waved but kept walking.

"Headed to *Tyrannosaurus*," she called across the space.

The cop nodded and kept muttering into his microphone.

When she got to *Tyrannosaurus*, the Chief of Police was standing by the hatch. Damn, he was freaking huge. Like two of her tall and four of her wide. Blackest skin she'd ever seen on a human. Scowling, but not working really hard at it.

Not yet.

"Something I should be worried about, Squire?" he rumbled at her as the mob got close.

Nyssa and eight armed sailors, like the beginning of a fairy tale. Or a bad joke.

"Captain Boru wanted us to increase security on the captured ship," she smiled up at the dark giant.

And leaving out the other bits. And some of the gear she'd packed.

"He expecting somebody to do something rash?" Chief Martinez

61

asked in a grumpy, put-upon tone. "My station doesn't have those sort of problems."

"He was worried that someone might try to steal it and sail it off," Nyssa lied. At least by omission. "Tasked us with guarding it closer until the auction. Then it isn't our problem anymore."

The man studied her closely. Big. Intimidating, except that she had two older brothers who were both big. Not as big as the Chief, but she'd been roughhoused as a kid. And had had to stare them down, too.

"You will contact me immediately, if there are any problems, Squire," he offered in one of those threatening tones that was just worse when he didn't put a threat behind it.

"Aye, sir," she agreed calmly.

Honestly, her brothers were probably still worse, but they were crazy. Chief Martinez didn't give off those vibes. Probably just as well.

He nodded and Nyssa keyed open the hatch. Folks inside knew she was coming, so they were standing in the cargo bay, armed and ready.

Nyssa ignored the big man and gestured her goons to board. Cam Farrell went last, scowling some unspoken threat to the Chief before she vanished.

Nyssa looked up at the man.

"I'm not planning on causing any trouble on your dock, Chief," she said simply. "Captain Boru sent me here with sufficient force that anyone else trying to cause it got crushed utterly before we handed them over to you."

He nodded. Perhaps placated for now. Perhaps not.

Nyssa stepped inside and closed the hatch. Farrell and Hoàng were both standing at the other end of the airlock with pistols in hand. She waved them off and considered the hatch.

"I need this locked," she said aloud. "And set so that an alarm goes off everywhere on the ship whenever the hatch opens. Or any of the other airlocks. Somebody handle that."

Farrell nodded. Nyssa didn't need to worry about most of the ship.

Just the electronic guts.

And whatever secrets they might hold.

16

———

Alex scowled as Jeremy entered his office.

"News?" Alex asked as the man settled in a chair.

"Yes, but not necessarily good," Jeremy replied.

"Talk."

"So, that's a cruiser hull," Jeremy acknowledged. "Old one, because we've got a note that *A'Zedi* is up to P-named hulls these days with new construction. And because that's a tug, they lost a good chunk of firepower out of the middle."

"And?" Alex prompted.

"And visuals still show a pair of heavy twin particle cannon turrets," Jeremy grimaced. "One forward and one aft. Four twin particle cannon turrets, more or less on the corners. If they stayed with the basic design, six missile tubes on the flanks, three and three. Way more firepower than *Hellhound* can take on, even if we were to surprise them."

Alex nodded. About what he'd figured. Far heavier than a frigate. Less than a true cruiser.

Way overpowered for someplace like Varfelis Station.

"This is where all that money comes in," Alex told his First Mate. "The funds that *Wronlori* has made available for us. We'll need to head back to Herli Station at some point and put up bounties and bribes for those folks to come down here."

"You don't think this *Marrakesh* is going to leave?" Jeremy asked.

Alex considered his First Mate. Not necessarily a friend. Pirates rarely allowed themselves such indulgences, especially because Jeremy Luna might be the top candidate to become captain if Alex's crew decided to get rid of him.

At the same time, they had moved beyond basic brigandry here.

"You need to know some things that I've kept secret up until now," Alex informed him, waiting for Jeremy to nod before he continued. "*Wronlori* is paying us to destabilize shit in this region. You know that much."

Jeremy nodded carefully now. Face and eyes a little askance.

"They want this place messy because at some point, they plan to drop a forward fleet base in the vicinity. Like here in orbit of Sybeth, or maybe over Ellarl. When they do that, they'll be in a position to open a new flank in their war on *A'Zedi*, as well as threaten all of those colony worlds of the interior who are trading with *A'Zedi* now."

"Where do we fit in there?" Jeremy asked.

"Varfelis Station remains in place," Alex nodded. "Civilian, because they'll need people sucking gas out of the giants, as well as mining minerals and ice and processing it. Mendoza and her people are too honest for the *Wronlori* folks paying us. *Wronlori* wants them out of the picture, or at least controlled, but they don't want to do it themselves. I got the impression, both from folks I've talked to as well as reading the news, that *Wronlori* is stretched about as thin as they can get, so they can't move a fleet out here anytime soon. Not without risking some other system. But they want shit stirred up."

"Like us blowing up an *A'Zedi* cruiser?" Jeremy hedged.

"They're stretched thin as well," Alex nodded. "No way they can send a fleet, either. Hell, I figure that tug is a spy of some sort, maybe scouting the area to see if they want to do the same thing *Wronlori* is planning."

"How do you know this, Alex?" Jeremy pressed.

"I got approached by a middleman, Jeremy," he replied. "They agreed to fund piracy in this sector, and we agreed to slip in and handle things when they do take over later. Guess you might say I'm also something of a *Wronlori* patriot, but they offered amnesty for me and all my people when it was done. You needed to know that part, but don't tell the mutts, because they might slack if they thought that

Wronlori would save their asses when this is all done. We gotta keep *A'Zedi* out. And everyone else. Keep the system destabilized but not destroyed, because I plan to be Governor, one of these days, ruling this place from my palace aboard Varfelis Station. Or maybe I have *Wronlori* build me an armed station so I can control everything."

Jeremy gulped once. Thought about it as Alex watched.

"So instead of pirates and brigands, we're really patriotic freedom fighters?" he asked with a scowl. "Hell of a way to ruin my lunch, Alex."

Alex laughed.

"You didn't think I wanted to be a pissant pirate for the rest of my days, did you?" he asked.

"No, but I had no idea we were getting ready to play in the big leagues either, boss," Jeremy replied.

"Then file that in the back of your head and get back to work," Alex ordered. "Now you know where we're headed over the next month or so, once we figure out what those punks on *Marrakesh* are up to. Then we'll bring in the big hammer and smash them."

Jeremy nodded and rose. Alex smiled as the man departed.

A'Zedi might think they could own this system, but they had another thing coming.

Alex Carson would see to that.

17

Nyssa was the only officer aboard, so she got everyone settled and ignored what the sailors had been doing when she interrupted. As long as they were alert while on duty.

Instead, she focused on a bag of gear that had been stashed in the first trunk. It got slung over her shoulder and settled.

"Anything in particular we should worry about, sir?" Trinh asked, smiling up at her.

"Nobody can get aboard without an alarm," Nyssa replied. "Nobody can get close to us on the outside without an alarm, either. Basically, I want to be a porcupine. Not attacking anyone but drawing blood on anybody who hassles us. Captain doesn't think anybody would make that mistake but doesn't trust the locals to behave because he doesn't know who the pirates are, since nobody is wearing name tags."

That got a laugh out of the group. She smiled.

"Past that, I'm taking over the captain's cabin here and then headed down to engineering to inspect the datacore," she continued. "See if I can do what I need to do or if I have to call for Coxswain Whelan or Carpenter Garber to come over and tear things apart."

"Would we be better off undocking and moving into a nearby orbit?" Cam asked.

Nyssa considered it. Thought better of it.

"No, because I might need to tear certain systems apart and would rather not worry about losing life support when that happens," she replied.

"Roger that," Cam said.

Nyssa got nods from the sailors, and they all moved to set up a harder defensive perimeter inside the ship. Later, they would sort bunks. Probably have to do a load of laundry and toss all the pirates' gear into a burn pile, if they were anything like the vids portrayed them.

She stopped at the hatch.

"Can someone take an hour and clean out my bunk?" she asked. "Strip the bed and add fresh sheets? All personal gear removed and tossed into a box somewhere to either be sold, disposed of, or turned in as evidence?"

"I'll handle that," Cam called.

Nyssa nodded and headed aft.

Smallish ship. Corridor down the center with engines and machines aft of a pair of cargo bays. Head and wardroom forward from that. Cabins and more storage forward still, with her new cabin just behind the bridge, from what she remembered of the layout.

She moved into engineering. Everything was generally shut down. A couple of generators humming, with life support on but still connected to the station directly.

Nyssa put her bag down and studied the various panels. She found a couple of plates from the manufacturer and confirmed that the ship had been built in a yard at Ranividi, part of the *United Technocracy of Wronlori*.

Long ways from home, but everything was, because she honestly would need to ask Zarah where the closest industrial shipyard was. *A'Zedi* kind of sat in the middle, with *Wronlori* to spinward and the *Holy Imperium of Copez* trailing. The *Enlightened Tyranny of Traisa* was rimward.

Varfelis was coreward and sideways spinward, midway between *A'Zedi* and *Wronlori*, with places closer to the core having been colonized over the last few centuries. They'd been in Monsanch recently, which was kind of close, at least in terms of nothing closer between here and there.

Lots of empty space in between.

She shrugged and dug out the owner's manual that Commander Messier had found. It was way out of date, since it didn't list weapons of any kind, but it held the basics that at least got her headed in the right direction.

Out of the bag came the socketdriver, and she backed out bolts to drop a panel and get into the computer systems that controlled the ship. Thing wasn't all that smart, but she wanted to be able to confirm that nobody had planted any bombs or such inside here. Physical ones. She had the tools to deal with logic bombs, once she plugged in some of the other toys she'd brought with her.

Noise behind her was Trinh making sure Nyssa heard her coming in.

"Everything good?" Nyssa asked.

"All set, Squire," Trinh replied. "Cam sent me aft in case you needed somebody tiny to climb inside something."

Nyssa laughed. She was average in height, with a slender build. At one hundred and fifty-five centimeters, Trinh was teeny.

"What are we looking for?" Trinh asked.

Nyssa pulled out a flashlight and aimed it into the electronic guts revealed.

"That is the main datacore," she said. "Navigation computer is above and a little behind that over here. Wanted to make sure nobody had booby-trapped the place."

"We looking for someone's bolt-hole, sir?" Trinh asked.

Nyssa's head snapped around. The woman grinned.

"Only reason you'd worry about those two being safe was if somebody might have forgotten to wipe their flight records," Trinh replied, eyes big and bright.

"You are correct," Nyssa nodded. "They didn't have a lot of time to do things when we dropped a hammer on them. And they hadn't emotionally recovered when Cam boarded with her team."

"Should we dismantle that, sir?" Trinh asked.

"I was just having that conversation with myself," Nyssa agreed. "Plus side, it gets it where I can dump all the memory out and store it in a backup. Downside, I'm not sure how hard it will be to put it all back together later."

"Lemme know if you need a ferret to get in there."

Nyssa nodded and considered. If this ship was a pirate, it must have come from somewhere. Those records should exist, even if someone tried to wipe them.

"Here," she handed Trinh the owner's manual. "I'm going to pull the datacore for analysis. You're in charge of navigating for me."

"Stand by," Trinh said, studying the charts. "We need a bucket to put bolts in."

The small woman looked around and found a small container.

"This should do," she said. "Got your pin driver?"

Nyssa held it up and triggered it once with a grinding whir.

"Okay, sir," Trinh nodded. "First set of bolts should be on the corners of the data controller, viewed from the top."

Nyssa held the pin driver with one hand and the light with the other as she leaned in and started to work.

18

Padraig greeted Captain Olafsson at the rear hatch. A bit more official than stopping by for a beer. Not a state visit.

"Permission to come aboard?" Olafsson asked formally, standing just on the other side of the line in the deck.

"Permission granted," Padraig nodded, holding out a hand that the big man shook.

Padraig had put on a clean uniform, but not done much more than that. Olafsson was a bit nervous but followed quietly as they headed inward to the wardroom.

Ships ran around the clock. Someone was always on duty. At the same time, the kitchens ran in pulses, serving food over a stretch of a couple of hours, then cleaning everything before starting the next batch of food.

Marrakesh was late in Padraig's day, so supper, while other crew members would be just having breakfast before going on duty.

As long as everything ran smoothly.

Padraig grabbed a tray and went down the line grabbing things. Olafsson did the same. Quirke had outdone himself, if only because everything looked like it had come out of the oven at the same time Olafsson had boarded, so it was all fresh.

Smelled wonderful.

He got a spot at a trestle table and sat Olafsson down across from him. They had one end, but nobody was immediately next to them.

Padraig knew that some captains were militant about dividing offi-cers and enlisted crew into separate spaces when they ate, but he had decided early on not to do something like that if he was ever in charge. Thus, there were two wardrooms and two kitchens, but they ran off-cycle to each other, and everyone was welcome to eat at whichever one was serving.

And it let him sit and gossip with the crew. Or hear dirty jokes. And it occasionally let crew members approach him with issues, ideas, or complaints, without necessarily having to make it official.

Often, you could quietly take someone aside and have a chat with them. Saved putting it down in their permanent record or having a Captain's Mast disciplinary session.

Padraig had found that his crew worked better this way.

Olafsson seemed a bit surprised at first, but relaxed as they ate. Padraig had chicken, cubed into a white sauce with steamed veggies. *Marrakesh* was going to be running out of the freezer and storage on this mission, because everything had to be imported to Varfelis. At the same time, he had a few prizes that he could swap with locals when he wanted to bribe someone. Fresh fruit, for instance. Or things from the various hydroponics he kept on the ship as they came ripe.

The wardroom could live without fresh for a few meals.

"I wanted to ask about piracy in general," Padraig began in a quiet voice.

Anyone within four or six meters could probably listen, but none of this would be state secrets. And it would help the crew understand better, since most of them spent their days going from food to duty to training to sleep.

"What about it, Captain?" Olafsson asked.

"You got lured out to Ecix to make a delivery?" Padraig asked. "Then there was nobody there except our four friends?"

"Aye," Olafsson grumbled. "Shoulda listened to my gut on that one, but they were offering cash. Lots of it. Half up front for a priority delivery. Fortunately, I still have all that cargo in my bay that I can sell at some point, so I'll come out ahead."

"What about the folks that spoofed you?" Padraig pressed.

"I'm pretty certain that somebody's account got hacked," Olafsson shook his head grimly. "Although, come to think of it, nobody has seen or heard from *Crazy Victoria* in a while. I thought they'd just been off mining. I'm guessing now that they got captured at some point and their credentials used."

"That would be my assumption," Padraig nodded. "Does anyone maintain any sort of inventory of the ships that come and go?"

"Station might," Olafsson shrugged. "'Course, not entirely sure them folks are all on the up-and-up, if you catch my drift. Probably an insider somewhere."

"What would happen if they were discovered?"

"Hmmm," Olafsson considered. "Depends on who, I suppose. Low-level nobody probably gets thrown in jail for a while then exiled permanently from the station. High level? Dunno."

Padraig nodded.

"Different topic for you," Padraig said. "How well do you know Abraham Ferrari?"

"Oily one, he is," Olafsson nodded. "Been sniffing around your ship, has he?"

"He wanted to go aboard the captured vessel and inspect it. Looking for an edge on everyone else."

"That would not surprise me in the least, Captain," Olafsson grinned. "That one's always poking."

"What's he do?"

"Buys and sells, Captain," Olafsson nodded. "Whatever it is you need, he can probably find it for you, for a price. And pretty good prices, but not so good that something automatically fell off a truck, if you catch my drift."

Padraig nodded. Stolen goods would be cheap, but they had to come from somewhere. And if you had a piracy problem, there would be a lot of goods floating around with unknown provenance attached.

"I'm given to understand that the ship we captured is a small freighter, as those things go," Padraig continued. "Not a miner by any stretch, but something that would haul cargo in and out. Your thoughts on selling it?"

"Station might want to bid," Olafsson replied. "Maybe make it a customs inspection boat. Or search and rescue. Others like Ferrari would buy it to expand their fleets of cargo haulers. I'm sure more than a few of them might be fronts for those pirates out there, but nobody's ever been able to verify anything."

"Any rumors of where the pirates are basing?" Padraig asked, watching the man closely now, since he'd had enough chance to get a feel for Olafsson's physical tendencies.

"Nothing anybody has ever told me," Olafsson replied with a chuckle. "But I'm just a scrap dealer and flatbed hauler. Too honest for most of those folks, I'm guessing."

Padraig nodded. That was the impression he'd gotten.

"Then I have a question for you, Captain," Olafsson continued. "Why is *Marrakesh* out here, anyway?"

Padraig considered all of the various sets of lies that had been prepared ahead of time for him by *A'Zedi Intelligence Services*, specifically for their questions.

"*A'Zedi* is more or less boxed in on three sides," he replied. "Coreward is the one place where we can explore, but this is an area that hasn't been surveyed in decades, at least by us. This ship was recently in Monsanch, which is closer to center on our axis, and a gateway to a cluster of colonies that direction. What's out this way? More importantly, could a place like Varfelis Station serve as a useful refueling and staging area, for those long-range scouts that head out looking for new places farther inward to put down colonies?"

"I see," Olafsson replied without any emotions.

It made perfect sense, from the *A'Zedi* side, but Padraig could see where the locals might not appreciate being drawn into the wars of the rim, such as they were. Or having organized militaries calling on a regular basis.

"What about you, Captain Olafsson?" Padraig spun the tables. "Are there worlds here in Varfelis that could be colonized?"

"The Iron Zone has nothing good," Olafsson shook his head. "Best-looking world is miles deep with gases in a runaway greenhouse. Caustic, toxic, high-speed deadly winds. No place to even land and build a dome."

"What about some of the moons around Sybeth?" Padraig pressed. "Why not put domes there and start growing food? Or put factories in orbit here, instead of processing gases to be hauled to *A'Zedi* or *Wronlori* worlds?"

"Money," Olafsson replied. "Those are expensive propositions, and nobody around here is that rich. Sybeth is on the outer edge of the habitable zone, but is also something of a brown dwarf, so it puts out more heat than it receives. But a dome costs a lot of money. Easier to bore down below the surface, but again, none of these moons are all that useful, except as real estate. If some major power were to move in, I presume that they could afford such a thing, but a lot of the locals would probably pick up stakes and move somewhere else if that happened."

He said that with serious eyes. Almost accusational.

Padraig nodded. Easy to see.

"As far as I know, nobody from my side is planning anything like that," he said honestly.

Because he had not been told anything along those lines.

"So why send *Marrakesh*, instead of something smaller?" Olafsson pressed.

"Nobody knew what to expect," Padraig replied. "We can take care of ourselves. Plus, as soon as we sell that captured ship, I plan to move to one of the giants and mine it. That lets us inject resources into the system to pay for everyone putting up with us. Trying to make friends."

Olafsson nodded.

"You've got one here, that's for certain," he said. "Being polite will make you more, especially if you keep the pirates to minding their manners while you're here."

"That we can do, Captain," Padraig smiled.

The man nodded and they went back to eating.

Padraig had made his case. And learned a few things.

Hopefully, he could use them to his benefit.

19

Kaitlin found it terribly amusing that her inquiries about renting a hall had turned into an invitation to meet with the station's mayor. At the same time, she supposed that *Marrakesh* would destabilize a lot of patterns just by being here. Throwing a party on top of that might be a bit much.

Thus, she had dressed nicely. Not in a uniform, because she was a retired civilian contractor these days, goddamnit. There was almost nothing mauve or mulberry in her closet on purpose. Instead, she was in green and maroon. Nice reddish slacks, with a mint blouse long enough to be a tunic.

Not a uniform, thank you very, **very** much. Retired.

Her smile as she was ushered into the mayor's office appeared infectious, as Madam Mendoza smiled back at her.

Kaitlin was used to the dark complexions of *A'Zedi*. Mendoza was almost as light as *Wronlori*. Somewhere in the middle. Short, with an average build. Intense eyes.

Kaitlin got her hand shook and set. Tea was chosen and steeping. Casual conversation.

Sure.

"How may I be of service, Mayor Mendoza?" Kaitlin asked formally.

"Call me Diana," the woman said. "This is not a police interview."

Kaitlin's smile redoubled. She'd wondered.

"Diana," she nodded. "I'm Kaitlin."

"You aren't in uniform?" Diana asked.

"I served for thirty years and retired," Kaitlin nodded serenely. "They were able to tempt me back, but they are paying civilian rates for my expertise, and I am not subject to military justice."

"He doesn't mind?" Diana asked.

"Captain Boru is one of the best captains I've ever served with, so it works out well," Kaitlin answered.

"I see," Diana replied. "So can I ask a question that might come off a bit rude and not offend you?"

"Certainly, Diana," Kaitlin nodded. She'd been expecting this, after all, as soon as the request came in.

"Why is *Marrakesh* asking about hosting what amounts to a cocktail party?" Diana asked.

Kaitlin's smile got huge.

"We have a captured warship to sell," she replied. "And no idea who the folks are who might want to buy it. Good guys, bad guys, whoever. Plus, we plan to be in system for a month or two, surveying and doing some mining, so we wanted to see who our neighbors would be."

"That ship is going to mine?" Diana asked.

"Indeed," Kaitlin agreed. "I'm Stevedore, so all that is my responsibility. We have a cargo module forward, and a Gas Transport module aft. That will let us drop down and suck up a lot of vapors to store. We don't have the most sophisticated tools to crack them down into constituent parts, but we can do some processing while we're there. Then Padraig plans to haul it all back here and sell it."

"Padraig?"

"Captain Padraig Boru," Kaitlin nodded.

"I see," Diana said, but Kaitlin could tell that she didn't. Not really. "And you'll only be staying for a month?"

"Maybe a bit longer," Kaitlin allowed. "This first mission was meant to see who lived out here, and how well they might take to improved trade ties back to *A'Zedi*. You're kind of in the middle of nowhere, but *Marrakesh* is a flexible ship to do lots of things, like surveying and gas mining. Plus, the folks back home like the captain. He's handled some pretty tough missions lately and impressed them."

"Oh?" Diana asked.

Kaitlin took an extra fifteen minutes to give the woman the highlights of the missions to Albany and Monsanch, without giving away trade secrets in the process. Better if the locals decided that Padraig was a nice guy here.

"That is most useful, Kaitlin," Diana said when Kaitlin finished. "Would it be better if the station hosted a general event, rather than you working on credit against sales and deliveries later?"

"It would," Kaitlin agreed. "We'll make good money, and have cash with us, but again, most of this was to meet and greet people in relaxed circumstances. If you wanted to host it instead, I don't think Padraig would mind one bit, although he might demand the right to make a contribution, since we'll have the budget already."

"Perhaps we'll split the costs, then," Diana nodded. "Would you be the person to contact for organizing?"

"Aye," Kaitlin said. "Me or Commander Chance Messier, *Marrakesh*'s First Officer. Padraig has put us in charge."

"And you wanted to do this before you had the auction?" Diana pressed.

"Meet buyers and talk," Kaitlin nodded. "We still need to identify a couple of inspectors and see which of them we want to hire for the sale."

"I can get you names of reputable folks," Diana nodded. "What's your schedule?"

"If we could do this in four days, that ought to give people time to organize," Kaitlin said. "And if we can get the inspection done before that, we can hand out results to everyone attending, then have an auction or sale in the next few days after that."

"A most interesting week, Kaitlin," Diana observed. "I'll put some people in my office directly into contact with you, and we'll get it moving."

"Thank you, Madam Mayor Diana," Kaitlin said, shaking the woman's hand. "We'd like to see what we can do to make this a nice place to do business."

"You and I both, Kaitlin," Diana said. "You and I both."

20

Nyssa was always surprised how small the actual memory components of a datacore were. The logic circuits and other bits were most of the volume, with a solid chunk of hardware no bigger than her fist at the center.

"That's it?" Trinh asked, staring at the hunk of black steel.

"That's it," Nyssa nodded.

"What are we doing next?" Trinh asked.

Nyssa grinned. The woman had basically attached herself as a side-kick here, but Nyssa wouldn't have known how technical Trinh was otherwise, although she supposed that all the certifications for weapons required a lot of technical expertise.

"Now, we dump it into this device," Nyssa said, pulling from the bag a gadget she'd gotten from her Intelligence contacts.

More than a clamshell computer, but not much larger. Packed to the gills with powerful tools, though.

Nyssa found the connectors and wired the mess together, sitting everything on a workbench as Trinh watched.

Nyssa turned to the woman.

"You didn't see any of this," she ordered the woman.

Trinh's eyes got big.

"Top secret stuff?" she asked.

"Two levels above that," Nyssa nodded.

Trinh nodded.

"Explains a few things," she said. "We in the spy business now?"

"I can neither confirm nor deny, Security Expert Hoàng," Nyssa replied. "You will keep your mouth shut if you don't want to get into a lot of trouble."

The small woman's mouth fell open, then she closed it and nodded.

Nyssa nodded back to her and started typing passwords. Took several to access this thing, because of what it was and who had built it.

Eventually, she got in and to a menu. Nyssa ordered the device to copy everything, then catalog it. She'd take that and start poking later, but her new tools would keep it clean.

After a few seconds, it beeped to draw her attention.

Nyssa nodded, then turned Trinh and smiled.

"They deleted everything," Nyssa said. "They think they did, anyway."

"Think?"

"Most systems delete the pointers, and not the actual data," Nyssa explained. "That actually takes a long time to accomplish. The stuff is still there, but the ship itself wouldn't be able to locate it. Here, I've got a lot of location and flight log data, all marked deleted, so I should be able to recreate everything. Plus, we want to scrub most of it before we sell it, anyway."

"We going pirate hunting?" Trinh asked hopefully.

"That's up to the captain," Nyssa replied. "But pretty soon, I'll be able to tell him where we might want to look."

21

Alex found it terribly amusing that *Marrakesh* and Mayor Mendoza had invited everyone to a party.

Everyone. Regardless of anything.

Briefly, he'd wondered if it was some sort of trap, but this was too good of an opportunity to pass up, and nobody in this system was currently looking for him. *Hellhound* always flew a different set of transponder codes when they went after victims.

Tonight, he'd dressed himself up nicely and left Jeremy in charge. Wandered the crowds, noting that there were at least a hundred folks standing around chatting and drinking, plus half that many in black with trays of glasses or serving troughs of finger food. Pretty good spread, too.

Marrakesh's crew was pretty obvious. All in mauve and black, with mulberry highlights. Military folks, when everyone else was either in whatever jumpsuit had the least stains on it, or their best going-to-Mosque gear.

Alex didn't stand out in this group, though he supposed that he looked more *Wronlori* than the invaders did. That darkness made them stand out around here, though few would comment on it.

He had a glass of wine in one hand but wasn't drinking more than the occasional sip. And every once in a while he would set it down and get a new glass, just so it looked like he was drinking as much as everyone.

Food he grazed. The mayor had hired a good catering shop for this.

Alex let the tide draw him close to the man in charge. Captain Boru, *Marrakesh*. He had a couple of obvious goons standing around, and there were others working the crowd. Nobody was armed, with Martinez enforcing that at the door.

He was safe.

Boru made eye contact as Alex got close.

"Enjoying yourself?" the man asked, holding out a hand. "Padraig Boru."

"Alex Carson," he replied. "Captain of *Hellhound*."

"Cargo or miner?" Boru asked, neatly separating this system into the two component parts that made the economy work.

"Cargo," Alex nodded.

He studied the man. Tall and somewhat lanky. Alex was average height, with a heavy build and long arms that had served him well when he needed to grapple or punch.

Boru didn't look like a brawler.

"Why is *A'Zedi* come to Varfelis?" Alex asked, noting that a couple of others nearby had all happened to lean in at the same time.

Too nervous to talk to the man? Alex never suffered nerves.

"Trade with the interior," Boru replied. "See if Varfelis is a good place to extend contacts and contracts for scouting beyond that."

Alex nodded. He wasn't the least bit about to believe a load of horseshit like that. *A'Zedi* could have sent one of those scouts. Instead, they'd sent a big, freaking warship. Not the mark of a peaceful people.

"What kind of cargo does *Hellhound* haul generally, Captain Carson?" Boru asked.

Alex shrugged, not about to offer this man anything remotely close to the truth.

"Whatever people hire me to carry," he replied.

As opposed to flight bays filled with six mismatched snubfighters. Six wouldn't be enough to take on an *A'Zedi* cruiser. Jeremy had been certain of that. Alex had already reached out to another pirate carrier that was pretty much a pair of secondhand *Wronlori* gunships with a frame to carry them on Ghostdrives.

"Where do you normally run?" Boru was asking.

Again, Alex shrugged.

"Nothing industrial or food related comes from Varfelis," he offered. "Usually, I run to *Wronlori* worlds on that border, generally hauling gas tanks in my bays."

"Ever run to Monsanch or the Plaquemines Region beyond that?" Boru asked. "We just came from there, and they are starting to develop medium and heavy industry."

Alex considered it. Much closer to *A'Zedi*. Much farther from *Wronlori*. No place he wanted to be, but if the money was good enough, maybe he'd need to start sending trade caravans that way when he was governor around here.

"Have not," he replied. "Wasn't ever worth it. You looking to build that network?"

"Not us," the man laughed breezily. "But someone could get really rich, once they figured out what a place like Monsanch needed."

Alex noted the nods around him, assuming that one of these dumbasses would actually take note and probably send a ship or two that way.

Maybe he needed to let the folks at Herli know, so they could post a few interceptors out there. Nobody around to know what happened, if your ship suddenly vanished off all scanners without having time to send a distress call.

"Useful to know, Captain," Alex offered. He held up his glass as if showing off how empty it was. "Need to go get more."

"Good talking to you, Captain Carson," Boru said.

Alex nodded and extricated himself as others slipped in to ask about Monsanch. He made a note of faces so he could follow up later with ships.

Someone would be dumb enough to try to work with *A'Zedi*.

In that case, they had it coming.

22

———

Padraig was exhausted as he collapsed onto his couch back on the ship and studied Chance.

She'd spent too much time at Headquarters, so parties like this were second nature to her. The woman looked like she'd just stepped from the shower into a new uniform. Padraig felt like he'd been keel-hauled under the bottom of a maritime ship.

"How can you be so fresh?" he asked.

Chance laughed.

"Nobody wanted to talk to me," she said with a grin. "And they stopped hitting on me when I started showing everyone pictures of Xandra and Daneel."

He laughed with her. The lonely Don Juans of this station would bounce off that front.

"Well, I was busy being genial," he offered. "What did you get from all of it?"

"Lots of folks showed up," she replied. "Ferrari and a cluster of folks that I gathered will likely be our bidders. Mendoza gave Kaitlin good names for the inspection, and we were able to pass out things to Ferrari and his friends. All in all, I think it went pretty well. Why, what did you see?"

"About a third were excited to see us," he nodded. "About a third antsy that *A'Zedi* might show up in force. About a third were there for free booze. About what I expected, but I'm not sure the best way to expand the good numbers."

"Not sure we can," Chance replied. "We're here, and we're going to upset lives just from that. Do you figure that your new bosses were expecting more than that from us?"

He eyeballed her closely. She and Kaitlin were in on the secret orders. They had to be, in order to make it work. At the same time, he and Nyssa were the only ones with the whole truth.

"I doubt it," he conceded. "Scouting the terrain was the mission. Whatever form that took, by giving us time to spend a month out here. We'll know more after that."

"What about *Tyrannosaurus*?" she asked. "Does it matter who buys it?"

"Not according to Mendoza, at least from what she and Kaitlin have talked about," he replied. "At the same time, I'm not sure if that frog has been boiling for so long that they don't realize it."

"Nyssa mentioned a long, slow rise in piracy," Chance nodded. "Will someone attack us?"

"That's why we have the Q-Module," he grinned harshly. "They might be expecting a low-end cruiser, when we really have the firepower of a Ship of the Line, at least briefly. More missiles would have been nice, but I don't expect we'd have to stand toe-to-toe with a mob of pirates for long. And next time, it will probably have to be a long-range scout frigate, instead of something smaller and not as well armed, but now they know that, too."

"How bad are we going to disrupt this system?" she pressed.

"Three-hundred-kilogram gorilla," he offered. "Just being here does things."

"And the things Nyssa learned?" Chance asked. "Were we likely to go inspect those coordinates?"

"Not by ourselves," Padraig shook his head. "That feels like the sort of pirate base we were looking for. *Marrakesh* can take care of itself, but that's too much like poking a hornet's nest, if you ask me. No, that would be where I would send an escort squadron. Lots of frigates designed for protecting themselves from these sorts of armed freighters while stomping on motherships. I can't imagine anyone has anything our size and capabilities. Don't get me wrong. I'd like to, but let's swap out for a pair of combat modules before we go down that path."

"Understood," she nodded. "Since I'm still fresh, why don't I take a few hours and review intelligence, plus write some things up?"

"You do that," Padraig grinned. "I'm going to crash for a while. Wake me after you send whoever it is packing with their tails tucked between their legs."

"Will do," she laughed, rising.

Padraig watched her go, happy again that he'd been able to get and retain the crew he had. And Madam Gelashvili had promised to bend a few rules to let him promote people when it was time, while not forcing them to take shore jobs or transfer out. He'd end up with some senior folks, but people he'd broken in just right.

Padraig had a feeling he would need that.

23

Chance found Nyssa Taggart working on the bridge, the only officer right now with Coxswain Whelan sitting in Padraig's chair in command. The Cox gestured as Chance entered.

"No, you keep it," she said. "Want to talk to Taggart for a bit first."

The Radio Officer looked up at her expectantly.

"In Padraig's office, I think," Chance nodded, leading her there.

She closed the hatch as they got settled.

"Sir?" Taggart asked.

"Been talking to the Captain," Chance said. "He wanted my observations about the party. I'm going to write those up, but I wanted your thoughts on some of the merchants and wheeler-dealers we saw there."

"Ferrari is exactly what everyone says he is," Taggart replied.

"Oh?" Chance felt her eyebrows rise.

"I might have penetrated some of his systems," Taggart nodded carefully. "Quietly. Man has a finger in just about every pie, but I can't find any evidence of criminal conduct beyond the usual smuggling one might expect. Nothing like the pirates we're looking for."

"Useful," Chance said. "What about the others?"

"Long spectrum towards criminality from Ferrari," Taggart replied. "And about half the folks at the party aren't actually based here at Varfelis. Mostly on the cargo side of the economy, coming and going, so I haven't been able to find anything tying any one ship to the problems. If we had a single candidate, we might be able to do something, but that's maybe fifty ships, and nobody stands out."

"What about the station?" Chance asked. "Are they legitimate? Or are they fronting for the bad guys."

"Hard to tell," Taggart grimaced. "I'm not really an expert on the topic, so I can't tell if we're seeing too much or too little, if that makes sense."

"It does, actually," Chance smiled. "And I have some experience there, so why don't you write down a few topics and I'll try to fill in some blanks."

"You?" The woman seemed surprised.

"I was on a desk for several years," Chance nodded. "Some of that was Personnel, but there was also a stint related to intelligence analysis. Or rather, looking at things and trying to find patterns. Might be able to find some here. Or at least help aim you."

"Oh, that would be most useful, sir," Taggart said. "Let me start gathering things and sending them your way. Been collating them for the Captain."

"Let him know I'm touching them as well, but you're in charge of that stuff," Chance said. "I'm merely helping out."

"Aye, sir," Taggart said. "Anything else?"

"Nope," Chance said. "Except that you're doing one hell of a bang-up job, Taggart, in case nobody has been telling you that."

"Thank you, sir." The woman rose and departed.

Chance took a few moments and considered the party. Nobody obviously good guys. No easy villains to identify.

Still, she had the feeling that things were on the verge of breaking.

Maybe it was time to think about raising the general alert level one?

If nothing else, the crew would need to remember that they weren't on vacation around here.

24

Padraig looked around his bridge with a smile. They'd sold off *Tyrannosaurus*, and Ferrari had indeed ended up owning it, for which Padraig was thankful. One less potential trouble spot to worry about, after Nyssa had briefed him about Ferrari's business files.

He had his first team with him today, which made sense. *Marrakesh* was about to do something they had all theoretically trained for, but nobody other than some of the newcomers aft with Kaitlin had ever actually done before.

"Radio, what is our perimeter looking like?" he asked, turning to look at Nyssa.

"We have a small flock of ducks with us, Captain," she grinned. "Rather more than statistical chance would predict."

"They know we're armed, Taggart," he nodded. "If they hang out at Alanta with us, the pirates are likely to leave them entirely alone, so I'm not surprised so many ships followed us from Varfelis Station. Keep a close watch on them, though. I'm expecting a couple of wolves in that mess."

"Aye, sir," she replied crisply.

"Speaking of," he turned to Maddox Nevin. "Guns, I would not be averse to stepping up your training routine. Keep the Q Module masked but have everybody do a couple of dry runs there, as well as cycling forward and practicing with the other teams. I want people sharp, just in case somebody decides to get stupid around here."

"Aye, sir," Maddox nodded. "Had been planning to ask you about that after we settled into orbit."

"Good man, Nevin," Padraig nodded.

He had a crew anticipating his orders in good ways. Prepared, and thinking ahead to how they could do things even better.

One of these days, most of his classmates were going to start sending him jealous hate mail over this crew.

Padraig let the grin light up his face.

"Helm, what is your status?" he asked.

Zarah Halloran still liked to laugh that she was three days out of Uni, because she had literally gotten her orders to report to *Marrakesh* on the third day after graduation. Since then, she had started to really blossom as an officer. He could see her taking command of her own boat in another decade or so, on her way to something big.

She paused and confirmed her boards, then flicked a switch and changed the main viewscreen from a forward view to an orbital animation.

"We're coming in fairly flat on this approach, sir," Zarah replied, her pale blonde hair bobbing as she nodded to some internal rhythm. "Technically, we're in the outer edges of the atmosphere now, but we'll be diving down and across once the Stevedore gives us the order. First pass is mostly to test for gravity anomalies and atmospheric density before we go too deep."

Padraig nodded.

"Radio, have you scanned the interior of Alanta yet?" he asked.

"Aye, sir," Nyssa replied. "Deep atmosphere slowly thickening until we reach some sort of liquid ocean at severe crush depths. Below that, it reaches a phase where all the carbon and metals have been compacted into a massive diamond, enclosing a magma core like a chocolate drop. Abraham Ferrari provided us with some standard mining charts and surveys others had done. I'm comparing those to my scans as we go."

"Keep us safe, Radio," he ordered. "There is nothing we need to accomplish today, or even this week."

"Roger that."

Padraig squared his shoulders and dialed a number aft.

"B-Module. Lynch."

"Kaitlin, you and Commander Schermer are on," he said. "Helm is standing by for flight instructions."

He leaned back and prepared to dive *Marrakesh* into the green atmosphere of Alanta for the first time.

95

25

***

Kaitlin turned to the Commander. Dana Schermer was a planetologist by trade, but still a naval officer. The woman grinned at her now and nodded.

Dana was a compact woman, similar to Kaitlin in many ways. In both cases, if you took perfectly average in almost all physical aspects, then squished her down ten percent to make her short and broad. Not fat. Not even heavy. Just broad in the shoulders and hips compared to Kaitlin's muscles.

Lots of brains in there, as the woman had a PhD and all manner of secondary initials after her name when you looked at her personnel records.

Kaitlin wasn't a scientist. She liked to think of her job as mostly a den mother for whatever strangers would come aboard when they swapped operations modules. Science, combat, or even mining.

A big part of her job was making people feel comfortable, and then teaching them the local dialect that had grown up on *Marrakesh*.

Dana Schermer had taken to all of it like a duck to water.

She glanced at a couple of boards nearby. Everything showing green.

"Bridge, this is Commander Schermer," she announced. "I am taking command for insertion. Stand by. Radio, I have previously transmitted a set of pressure ratings for depth. You'll be in charge of calling as we cross levels down. Helm, you have the initial course as plotted, but understand that those pressure ratings are estimates. Plus, there will be storms brewing around us, since we didn't come in on the poles. Better safe than sorry, but none of today's pass is intended to do anything more than train you folks in the fine art of gas wildcatting. All hands, stand by."

Kaitlin liked the way the woman was grinning as she spoke, like this was all some vast practical joke on the universe. But then, *Marrakesh* was a cargo carrier, not a warship or a scientific exploration vessel. A jack of all trades.

"Helm, are you ready to dive?" Dana asked.

"Helm, ready for insertion," Zarah Halloran replied smoothly.

"All ahead ten percent on the rotary thrusters," Dana ordered. "Down plane ten degrees. Radio, call the depth readings."

Kaitlin found that she was holding her breath, but nothing was really happening. *Marrakesh* had nosed over and was slowly descending into the atmosphere. On the forward view, she could see the green and gold cloud tops suddenly fill the skies as they were sliding down a ramp.

It was like landing in a shuttle through a thunderstorm, without the lightning because they had located a calm, quiet spot to do this. In the distance, she could just make out other birds flying, but each of those was another ship, dropping down to vacuum up gases.

All of them were likely to fill their tanks before *Marrakesh* returned to the station, but they weren't here pursuing financial benefits for themselves, so it wouldn't matter that the market was somewhat flooded with product from Alanta by the time *Marrakesh* returned.

Plus, Dana assured her that they could dive deeper than anybody else, because *Marrakesh* was built like a warship, while the others were civilian stuff.

Plus, none of them had planetologists aboard.

"Radio, first layer descent completed, all readings normal," Nyssa Taggart said over the quiet line.

"Maintain course and heading," Dana replied.

They dropped into clouds now, but none of this was water. Or rather, water plus about ten thousand other things, swirling around them like cotton candy at several hundred kilometers per hour.

The sky vanished and the view got darker, occasionally brightening as the first layer of clouds wasn't solid.

"Helm, bring up all running lights to maximum intensity," Dana ordered.

Outside, the clouds got brighter as *Marrakesh* began to glow. Kaitlin had to close her jaw because it had fallen open. Dana's grin never slackened.

"Approaching second layer marker," Nyssa called after a bit.

"Engineering, what is our status with pressure and power?" Dana asked.

"Engineering, I'm showing all greens on my systems. Outside pressure is rising steadily, but I'm not showing any warning markers anywhere."

And Kaitlin had no doubt that Knight Ahearn—Jareth—was eyeballing everything sharply as they did this. *Marrakesh* was his baby, in ways that only Padraig exceeded.

"Helm, hold us at the second layer marker," Dana ordered. "Maintain forward velocity, but level us off there and keep an eye on the barometer as storms run."

"Level and forward, aye," Zarah replied. "We have leveled off at the current pressure rating."

"Now, boys and girls, the fun starts," Dana said with a cackle that had Kaitlin grinning just as much. "Helm, begin your roll to starboard. One-eight-zero and hold."

"Starboard one-eight-zero and hold," Zarah replied. "Stand by."

The screens were showing clouds, but Kaitlin could see the inversion as the clouds shifted around. *Marrakesh* was turning turtle, which was something that they had to do, since they weren't designed for this.

The modules plugged in from the top like humps on a camel. Two of them, most of the time.

"Wildcat crew, stand by to deploy your hoses," she said.

Above them—or below them, depending—a team of Dana's folks were standing by with rolled up hoses a kilometer long on tremendous spools.

"Anytime you're ready, Dana," one of her men replied over the line.

"Helm, are we stable?" Dana asked.

"Stable, aye," Zarah replied. "Bit bumpy, but that's just me getting used to flying upside down."

Dana laughed.

"A normal ship would have everything ready to point down and deploy that way, Helm," she said. "We're gonna have more fun this way."

"If you say so, Commander."

Kaitlin laughed. Dana was a laid-back woman, so she had fit in well with this crew.

"Wildcat crew, begin deploying your hose."

Kaitlin listened as the spools turned, a quiet rumbling sound she felt more with her feet than her ears.

Another advantage, in addition to being able to dive deeper than most gas miners. They had about four times as much hose, and that all brand new from the factory. Most ships only carried a few hundred meters of line, so that limited the depths they could reach.

Marrakesh was set up on this mission to get down a ways and pull up stuff that maybe didn't bubble up to the surface all that often. Should be worth more to the locals.

Always a benefit.

"Gas lines at maximum hang, Dana," the man said.

Dana reached out a mauve-painted nail that matched her uniform and pressed a button. Machines started to rumble around them.

"We are now mining gas, people," she announced proudly. "All hands, watch your gauges and your responsibilities, but you have just officially gone into the wildcatting business."

A few cheers over the line, which just made Dana grin all the more. And it was infectious.

Kaitlin watched the first tank pressurize from empty. They weren't going to fill everything today, as this was both a proof of concept for the crew, as well as a training exercise. Still, it filled pretty quickly. And they had seven more tanks to go later.

The wait was both interminable, and over all too quickly.

"Wildcat crew, stand by to stop pumping," Dana finally announced, causing Kaitlin to almost sigh.

The woman pressed a button and one of the quiet hums died away.

"Wildcat team, begin recovery operations," Dana called.

More hums as the spools wound that hose back into the ship, before silence fell.

"Helm, this is Commander Schermer," Dana got serious. "Reminding you that we are flying inverted, and that a down planes command takes us up and out of the atmosphere. Confirm your readiness."

"Helm, ready to dive," Zarah replied quickly.

"Down planes ten degrees and ahead twenty percent on thrusters," Dana ordered crisply.

"Down ten. Ahead twenty. Stand by."

Dana turned to her and leaned close enough to whisper.

"Next time, we'll actually roll over normal, but I wanted to make sure they were prepared for things to be weird," Dana said. "Flying like this is always a novelty for most crews."

"Completely insane," Kaitlin assured her, which just caused the woman to grin all the more.

"Radio, call levels as we ascend," Dana spoke up again.

"Approaching first layer now, sir," Nyssa replied.

"Helm, let's get silly," Dana decided. Kaitlin almost cringed. "Begin a starboard roll, one-eight-zero, flattening and reversing your planes as you go so that we continue our ascent."

Kaitlin wasn't sure about the look on her face, but Dana's grin just got bigger.

"One-eight-zero and ascending, aye," Zarah said nervously.

Kaitlin could hear the twinges in Halloran's voice now, but it didn't crack. Concentration. Focus.

Plus, Padraig was watching and could override anything as they went.

"Clearing first layer and ascending," Nyssa called.

"Helm, ahead one quarter and insert us into a standard orbit," Dana said. "Captain Boru, you have command."

Kaitlin needed some coffee after all that. Completely new. Utterly strange.

Really, really fun.

This sort of thing was the only reason they'd been able to talk her into coming back to work on a starship.

26

Alex didn't really hate the kinds of folks that Herli Station represented, but he could see some future date when he had to lead a squadron of warships in here to either smash the place entirely to rubble or conquer it and annex it to his future government at Varfelis.

It was one thing to have pirates running around causing trouble for other people. And he was one of those troublemakers. At the same time, when it was his turn to become the law, he was going to have to make sure that his grip was more solid.

For now, *Hellhound* was docked, and he'd had Jeremy run an inventory of the other ships in port. *Anteater* was here. As was *Hermes Multistellar*. The former wasn't exactly a warship but was a retired revenue cutter that was built sturdier than most. The latter was really a shell that contained a pair of old *Wronlori* gunboats with a better Ghost Drive and space for the crews to relax between raids.

And his old buddy Adrianna Velazquez was present, in her own escort carrier like *Hellhound*. Alex wondered if he'd end up having to fight a duel with the woman. Or win a drinking contest.

Bad *juju*, but it was what it was.

He and Jeremy were at the aft lock. Alex settled a disruptor on his hip and shrugged once to settle everything. He didn't figure any of his enemies were desperate enough to jump him here, but he also didn't feel like walking around with a bodyguard, lest folks start whispering that he was getting old and nervous.

Forty would be here soon, and not a lot of captains lasted long after that birthday, unless they were among the very best. Alex would deal with that when it arrived.

For now, he had a mission in mind. And a lot of funds under the table to recruit yahoos and hooligans to help.

"You're in charge until I get back," Alex ordered his First Mate. "Crew will get leave spread over several days, but I want to know what the locals have to say before I commit. Keep them sharp. And if I call for help, arrive shooting."

"Understood, boss," Jeremy replied with a sharp nod. "Most of them aren't cowards, at least last time I checked, but make sure Adrianna doesn't punch you in the gob."

"Oh, I prolly got that one coming," Alex laughed. "But only one. Then she has to listen, or I'll knock her ass down and kick her a few times."

Jeremy laughed back. He understood that history. Alex shrugged.

Shit happened in this business.

He exited the lock and found himself on the main station concourse.

Herli Station followed a pretty standard design. Main ring with the docking locks around the middle. Levels up and down from there, but none stuck out as far, to allow ships to attach themselves.

Not as much cargo capacity as Varfelis Station, because it was generally more of a meeting hall than a warehouse. And no refinery, because Herli was a brown dwarf that had been ejected from some nearby star system in the not-too-distant past. Maybe a million years or so. Solo wanderer, which also described a lot of the pirates that came through.

Alex made his way to a particular bar/lounge/dive that catered to captains and first officers. Quieter, with no live entertainment and benches attached permanently to trestle tables, instead of things that could be swung in a brawl. It was also more of a coffee shop than anything, where bankers and middlemen often hung out to make deals or buy hijacked cargo cheap.

He entered and several people eyeballed him as he crossed to a particular spot and stood facing Adrianna Velazquez. There was a table in the way, so she'd have to climb over it to punch him. That or just draw and open fire.

From the look on her face, she had already done the geometry in her head as he walked up.

"Carson," she growled, a mug of coffee in one hand. That probably kept her from shooting him.

"Velazquez," he nodded carefully. "You available for hire?"

Several other heads snapped around at that. Loaded language around here. Especially since *Velazquez* the ship wasn't a cargo ship. No, Adrianna's boat was a carrier like *Hellhound*, though she only had five mismatched snubfighters last time he'd checked. *Hellhound* at least had six. Small difference, but a niggling edge. Like glass fibers under your fingernails.

Her jaw came up and out.

"Maybe," she offered. "What fool gave you money?"

Alex grinned.

"You wouldn't believe me," he countered.

"Try me," she snapped.

Alex let his gaze wander a bit. Adrianna wasn't an ugly woman. Rather attractive, when you got right down to it. Darker hair like those *A'Zedi* punks. Redder skin, but still dark. Skeleton lean, though. Skin wrapped over barbed wire and animated by hungry rage. Aggressive in bed, the few times they'd locked horns on the topic, but not all that much fun in the end.

Going different directions in life.

He brought his eyes back to hers.

"I need a ship killed," he announced simply.

Then Alex looked up and speared two other captains he knew: Yavin Nicolau off *Anteater*, and Porter Nyseth, commanding *Hermes Multistellar*.

"They're a pretty big ship, too," he continued, letting the suddenly silent room listen in. "An *A'Zedi* tug that's probably a spy ship at Varfelis."

"*Marrakesh*," Yavin replied quietly, showing that he'd either been through there in the last week or two, or had talked to folks who had.

"That's right," Alex said. "*Marrakesh*. Cruiser hull. Frigate firepower. Somebody is paying me to make sure they never make it home, but *Hellhound* can't take them by itself. Figured I'd hire some pirates for the task, because I don't figure any of you would like it if *A'Zedi* dropped a forward base around here. Even just for mining the Varfelis system."

He nodded to the publican.

"Coffee for me," he said, then went ahead and sat down across from Adrianna uninvited.

Close enough she could slap him. Or punch him. Or even kiss him.

You never knew with a woman like her. Definitely not somebody to take for granted.

Nearby, both Yavin and Porter had risen and were making their way over. A few other captains might be listening, but they wouldn't join the conversation without an invite, and Alex wasn't about to bring in random folks unless he didn't make any progress with his first three choices.

"You available for hire?" he repeated to Adrianna in a friendlier voice.

"What's in it for me?" she asked smoothly.

You never knew with her. Money might be enough. Or maybe a kilo of flesh. Or a few liters of blood.

"Cash up front," Alex replied. "Half now. Half escrowed. Pillage at Varfelis after smashing an *A'Zedi* warship into the mud. What does a woman like Adrianna Velazquez want?"

Her eyes danced with things that didn't look pleasant, but this was the flip side of taking money and turning himself into a *Wronlori* patriot.

Plus, if he did end up causing *Anteater*, *Velazquez*, and *Hermes Multistellar* to be used up in the process, that was three fewer folks competing with him later when he went ahead and took over Varfelis.

Yavin and Porter joined before he had to rise to Adrianna's bait, which was probably for the best.

This industry really wasn't big enough for both of them.

Padraig was in his office, studying the latest intelligence that Nyssa had organized for him, both the basic stuff that came with being the Radio Officer, as well as the quiet things that she got when folks left a hatch unlocked somewhere, however metaphorically.

It didn't add up. Or rather, it did, but not in ways that really left him all warm and fuzzy inside.

Marrakesh had flown to Alanta as part of a fairly massive convoy of small ships, acting like something of a lifeguard as they all dove deep to wildcat. Like sea birds hunting the little fishies below.

Since then, Kaitlin and Dana Schermer had taken their time about filling the tanks aft, pausing after each run to do some preliminary cracking with the small refinery, then venting off the stuff that everyone else would be hauling back when they filled from shallower levels.

Based on FOB prices at Varfelis Station, he might technically even show a profit for this mission, which was simply weird to think of. Warships were expensive beasts, which was why so many of the ships around them were so much more fragile, and so thinly crewed compared to what he had.

However, the economy around here would be greatly stimulated by the sorts of gases he would be delivering. Already, there were a couple of larger tankers sitting close to Varfelis Station, seemingly waiting for his load. And while they would technically be hauling things to *Wron-*

lori ports, and thus were enemy vessels under certain sets of assumptions, they were neutrals in a neutral port, so he couldn't say anything.

Hell, those captains might even be laughing at the prospect of an *A'Zedi* warship supplying *Wronlori* industry with some of the things he had.

Couldn't be helped. Quite literally, the cost of doing business around here.

But the covey of little quail running around had all meandered off over the last few days.

Viewed one way, they had all come, filled their gullets with food, and were returning to the nest to feed the hatchlings.

Padraig was feeling a bit more paranoid than that. Part of him was wondering if the folks he'd smashed when they first got here two weeks ago had finally had a chance to get themselves reorganized.

Maybe come for a little payback.

He keyed a number aft.

"B-Module. Lynch."

"Kaitlin, it's Padraig," he said. "When you have a chance, can you ask Commander Schermer about those last two tanks she wanted to fill?"

"Sure," Kaitlin replied. "She's right here. Hang on."

"What can I do for you, Captain?" Dana asked.

"We've filled six of eight at this point," he began. "All useful stuff, based on your reports. What would it change about our final delivery to Varfelis if we paused here and moved our wildcatting out of Annan?"

"The ice giant?" Dana asked.

"Correct."

"We'd be going deeper into the ammonia range, for one," Dana replied. "Nothing that would be bad for the hull, but it might end up either staining the exterior a more bluish color, based on some of the trace elements floating around, or it might scour you right down to the original finish on the hull metal that the solar wind had dulled and ionized. Any particular reason?"

"I don't like being predictable, Dana," Padraig replied. "And all those ships we've been escorting have, for the most part, returned to

Varfelis Station at this point. Do we benefit or cost ourselves by shifting our point of operations?"

"Benefit, I think," Dana said. "We're bringing in a bunch of stuff that's fairly exotic around here and shifting to Annan lets us expand that range greatly. How soon did you want to move, Captain?"

"How soon would your team be ready, Commander?" he countered.

"We were planning to make the next run after lunch, so we can easily delay that a day," Dana offered. "Might spend today catching up on some of the maintenance tasks we've been putting off, if you give the word."

"You go ahead and take the day," Padraig decided. "I'll let my people know, and we'll transition shortly."

"Aye, sir," she said.

Padraig cut the line and felt a major weight seemingly slide from his shoulders. Like he'd been anticipating trouble, but now it would have to find him instead of dropping out of Ghost-space on top of him, like he'd done when rescuing *Delilah*.

He nodded and rose, making his way to the bridge.

Zarah Halloran was in charge right now, so he moved to his station and smiled at her when she looked up inquiringly.

"Question," he said to get her focused. "That set of coordinates that we pulled from the logs of *Tyrannosaurus*. What's there?"

"Astronomical survey says it is a brown dwarf, Captain," Zarah replied. "Too small to ignite fusion, but larger than any of the giants around here by about a factor of four. Records don't show any planets, but there is some sort of station there, because *Tyrannosaurus* came and went to those coordinates several times over the last two years."

Padraig nodded. Much as he wanted to slip over there and look, he had a pretty good idea how bad of a mistake that would be. At least without a bunch of heavily armed friends. Still, marking it as a pirate base in his head helped.

"I want you to keep an Aetherial sensor pointed at that vector at all times going forward," Padraig ordered. "Log that for whoever is in charge and the Radio folks."

"We expecting an attack from that direction, sir?" she asked.

"To be honest, I am," he nodded. "I would greatly enjoy it if my paranoia was getting the better of me, but we don't lose anything for being extra prepared, because any trouble that is coming will likely come from there."

"Understood, sir," she nodded. "Logging that now. Any other orders?"

"Affirmative, Halloran," he grinned. "Prepare to break orbit and plot me a course to the ice giant Annan. We're going to shift our mining operations there immediately."

"Aye, sir," she said, obviously caught off-guard but quickly rallying. "Break orbit and lay in a course for Annan. Stand by."

He smiled and watched her work quickly. And it was quick. She had sure hands typing.

"Course laid in and ready for you, sir," she announced.

"All hands," he announced on the ship-wide. "Stand by for Ghost-space as we move *Marrakesh* to a different fishing hole."

He nodded to Zarah.

"Break orbit, then transition to Ghostdrives as soon as we're clear," he ordered.

On the main viewscreen, the greens and golds of Alanta dropped from sight, replaced by a vast starfield of diamonds on black velvet. Then that shift as they moved out of this plane to Ghost-space itself, another vibrational existence where the laws of physics were different.

He hadn't given her any suggestion that they hurry, so they crossed the space at a slow FTL, taking fifteen minutes to arrive.

Padraig wondered about all those ships that had been hovering safely around *Marrakesh*. He could have told them where he was going. Maybe invited them along.

At the same time, that brown dwarf loomed big in his mind, and he wondered which of the ships hanging out at Alanta with him were scouts for the pirates.

He doubted that all of them were innocent.

And better this way, to keep everyone on their toes.

He pulled up the roster and checked the schedule, then dialed a number.

"Forward Wardroom."

"Is Squire Taggart having lunch?" he asked.

"Stand by," the man replied. A few moments passed. "She's in line now. Do I need to pass a message?"

"Negative," Padraig said. "I'll join her shortly."

They had arrived at Annan.

Padraig felt the need for some spy games.

28

Nyssa had just settled with a tray of food when she saw Captain Boru enter the wardroom, making his way directly towards her.

She asked a few silent questions with her face as he approached, but he indicated that she should remain seated. Still, she grabbed a spork and started shoveling, just in case.

Captain sat with a wry grin as she paused to drink some reconstituted juice and choked a little.

"Sir?" she asked.

"You eat," he said. "I'll talk."

Nyssa nodded.

"We've just changed orbits from Alanta to Annan," he said.

Nyssa nodded. She'd heard the announcement while finishing up getting dressed before breakfast.

"There is a new standing order for Radio to keep long-range watch on that brown dwarf we have designated as a pirate base, on the assumption that trouble will be coming at us from that direction, and I would like as much extra warning as I can get."

Again, she nodded and shoveled, chewing and swallowing as quickly as she could in case this was leading to something that would take priority on everything else.

There had been a lot of those lately with her new responsibilities.

Captain Boru got serious now as she watched.

"I did not warn anybody at Alanta that we were leaving," he

continued. "Nor did I tell them where we were headed. There are ships in orbit of Annan, but I want you to start cataloging who follows us. And then, when you find somebody suspicious, I want you to turn your intellectual and technological firepower loose on them to see why. Am I clear?"

"We assuming pirate scouts, such as the ones that set up Captain Olafsson and *Delilah*, sir?" she asked.

"Precisely that, Squire," he nodded. "We look like a standard Tactical Transport here, with cargo and mining modules. That means that we would be in the range that a swarm of pirates could attack and possibly destroy, if they were of a mind to."

"Why would they do that, sir?" she pressed.

"Your notes on the sudden but continual rise in piracy around here, Nyssa," he replied. "To me, that looks like a deliberate thing. Boiling the frog slowly, to use the ancient fairy tale. And Intelligence Operations sent us here, so I am assuming that they suspected certain things, but weren't in a position to confirm them. Given the stellar geography, problems here would likely be caused by *Wronlori*, softening up this corner so that they might invade and occupy this region and give them a stepping stone towards all those interior colonies that are currently too far away to reach easily."

"We going to stop them, sir?" she pressed.

"Not our problem, Nyssa," he nodded. "If I thought we could slip away cleanly, I'd head to Varfelis Station right now and dump our load before heading home, but that would look like we'd been spooked, given our original announced itinerary."

"Ah, so they might be counting on us to stay at Alanta?" she asked. "Were counting on it, and now we're elsewhere."

"Exactly," he nodded. "Plans that have been made will have to be adjusted, so you will birdwatch for whoever is paying too much attention to *Marrakesh* and warn me and Chance, so that we can be prepared to handle it, whatever it turns out to be. And if you have to adjust your time as Radio Officer, let me know so we can get some more folks cross-trained to handle basic traffic."

"Bex Magorian and some of the others are doing exceptional," she nodded. "And Glen Tameron might be getting close to the sort of qualifications that earn him a promotion."

"Good," Captain Boru said. "We'll be in a position to let folks have extra stripes and remain aboard in their current positions, so they will have an advantage if they decide to transfer to another boat later on. Keep me posted about Magorian and Tameron."

"Anything else, sir?" she asked.

"You're keeping me several steps ahead of everyone else," he said with a nod. "Keep it up."

Nyssa nodded back. Captain Boru smiled and rose, departing without another word.

She still felt like something of an impostor, but that was being almost the youngest member of the crew, and the youngest officer by far. Still, Captain Boru believed in her. As did some really scary people back at Horwin, so she must be doing something right.

Nyssa went back to shoveling and started planning how she might break into some of her neighbors, once she was certain who was up to no good.

29

Kaitlin was aft with Dana, two mugs of hot chocolate, and all the boards showing everything that the woman might need as they prepared to dive into an entirely new planetary atmosphere.

While Alanta had been primarily seen as greens and golds, both from orbit and when you dropped down into it, Annan was a blue world, with hints of purples that showed up in storms, where vortexes pulled things from the deepest depths and then swirled them around in a cyclone before releasing them to the deep again.

"How big is that storm?" Kaitlin asked, touching the screen as one of the big ones went by underneath them.

Dana checked the system and whistled.

"About two thousand kilometers across the eyewall," she said. "And calm, too. Annan is doing a lot of churning around that, but the center isn't moving more than a few hundred kilometers per hour. That eyewall might be approaching a shear of six thousand kph."

"Anybody ever mine something like that?" Kaitlin asked.

Dana laughed.

"*Marrakesh* isn't sturdy enough to survive it," she said. "Most civilians would be tin cans under truck wheels if they got close."

"Huh," Kaitlin grunted.

"Why?" Dana asked in a tone that dragged it out to about four syllables.

"All that purple," Kaitlin replied. "Stuff pulled from the depths.

Probably pretty rare in those sort of concentrations. Was wondering if there was a way we could somehow take advantage of that."

Rather than answer, Dana studied her for a moment, then started typing.

"Bridge. Taggart."

"Radio, I need a hard, directed scan at the storm I'm sending you coordinates for," Dana replied. "Please light it up with everything you have, then wash it through my meteorology software and let me know when you have results."

"Affirmative, Commander," Taggart said. "Stand by."

Marrakesh didn't ping or anything. There were no rumbles indicating more generators being brought online to handle the scanner request. What Kaitlin did see was a mass of data and the image of the storm suddenly got so incredibly razor sharp on the monitor that she could see smaller eddies inside the larger whirlpool. Golds, crimsons, and even blacks that were some gas, instead of a vacuum.

"Data coming in now, Commander," Taggart said after a few minutes. "Is this sufficient?"

"It should be, Radio," Dana replied. "Thank you. I will analyze and let you know if I have other requests, but this should be what I needed."

She cut the line and Kaitlin watched the woman's grin widen.

"This is where it gets a little hinky," Dana said, using one of those specialist, technical terms that could mean just about anything you needed it to. "We could sit off on this corner here, above and trailing the storm some. The ride might be a little rough, but we ought to be able to hover above the point where those clouds inflect and start inward. If you look right here, they come up, hit a certain altitude, and go almost perfectly sideways as they get sucked across before plummeting down again."

Kaitlin had gotten a crash course in meteorology during this mission, so she was able to adjust the view, showing the storm now from the side, like a top spinning across the floor. She could see what Dana was referring to.

"Why is it so square?" she asked.

"Barometric pressure," Dana nodded. "Whatever is driving the storm only has enough energy to pull this stuff to a certain level, where it is suddenly too dense to be drawn higher. It's almost rain, when you look at it, though the spectrograph shows almost no water in that. Still, liquid."

"Valuable?" Kaitlin asked.

Dana brought up a different screen.

"These are the prices for things at Varfelis, as of yesterday," she said. "That's probably what we're looking at here."

"Liquid gold," Kaitlin nodded. "Granted, nobody uses gold as the basis of an economy, but still."

"Agreed," Dana said. "That's some valuable stuff, mostly because nobody is probably configured to do this. Nor crazy enough to try."

"Are we?" Kaitlin asked.

Instead of answering, Dana types a number on her console.

"Bridge. Boru."

"Captain, I'm sending you the data we've gathered on the storm below us," Dana said.

"Got it," Padraig said quickly. "What am I looking for?"

"Note the pressure indications at a spot roughly seven to eight hundred meters above the trailing edge tops."

"Almost calm, Dana," he replied. "You and Kaitlin planning to drop your wellhead into that and draw out the purple stuff?"

"That is an option, Padraig," she replied. "The local industrial value would be exceptional. In spite of who might be taking advantage of it."

"We can always come back for more for ourselves before we head home," he replied. "And fill all eight tanks instead of just the last two we have available. I take it you'd like to try now?"

"Affirmative, Captain," Dana replied. "The storm is stable, and we have as much data as we can get right now."

"Stand by, ladies."

Kaitlin nodded at Dana's sudden confusion. The geologist didn't really get Padraig, for all they'd relaxed enough to be on first name basis. Dana wouldn't see this next step coming, but it was obvious, at least to Kaitlin.

"All hands, this is the captain," Padraig's voice filled the room as he hit every chamber. "Report to duty stations. This is not combat, but we are about to sail into danger. Repeat, sailing into danger, so everybody stand by for rough weather ahead.”

Kaitlin laughed. Padraig sometimes sounded like some old salt on a planetary sea in a vid, in spite of commanding a starship. At the same time, there would be weather coming. Sort of.

Enough to probably warrant waking folks and getting his top team into position, instead of whatever enlisted folks had duty at this moment.

He was back a moment later.

“Dana, Kaitlin, if you’ll give me fifteen minutes, we’ll be set,” he said. “I’m going to take a quick biobreak. I suggest you do the same.”

Kaitlin nodded. Dana finally understood. *Marrakesh* wasn’t a front-line cruiser. She was still an *A’Zedi* warship, crewed by some of the sharpest folks Kaitlin had ever had the privilege to serve with.

It might be science, but they were going to approach it professionally.

And it was likely to be fun.

30

Padraig had buckled himself in, just because that extra step served to focus the mind. Like that ancient saying about a good hanging in the morning.

Ten minutes, and he had everyone he wanted at their stations, a few still a little sleepy and bedraggled, but that was life in the navy. Sometimes, shit happened on its own schedule, and you simply had to deal with it then, rather than when your duty schedule came up.

Nyssa was bright. Zarah had been studying. Maddox was sucking down coffee to wake up, but Padraig really hoped that he didn't need the guns for anything today. Not much *Marrakesh* could do against a hurricane that big.

"Radio, we're going to be pushing the envelope a little today, so I want you to launch a probe and center it about a thousand kilometers above the eye of the storm, geosynchronous to move with it until we retrieve it later," he began, turning to Nyssa. "As you bear."

"Stand by for probe launch," she nodded, typing furiously. "Should we warn everybody off?"

"Is there anybody close?" he asked.

"Within our visual horizons, yes, but nobody that close to our current flight path, no, sir," she replied.

"Issue a general warning to stay clear as we navigate, but don't spell out the details," he ordered. "Then have the probe mark a perimeter and warn us if anyone crosses that line."

"Aye, sir," she said. "Probe launching now."

Padraig nodded. Crisp. Sharp. Professional. He'd been wrong before, thinking she might never have command of her own boat. However, it would be a spy ship, not a line cruiser, and she'd be amazing at it.

His job was making sure she was ready for every facet of command when she got there.

He turned to Maddox next.

"Might be worth having your teams running some exercises while we're inverted and pinched against a storm where we can't maneuver, Guns," Padraig continued. "But hopefully, we won't need you."

"Training exercises, aye," Maddox smiled. "Sounds like fun."

And it probably would be. Maddox was excellent as a gunner. He'd be the first one to have a line command, one of these days, most likely.

"Helm, Commander Schermer is going to roll us over and sail us down over the top of that storm, close enough that we can siphon stuff churned up," he said. "Less margin for error here than before, so you and Nyssa stay in constant touch and make sure that you both have backups shadowing you aft if we suffer any sort of mechanical issues. Understood?"

"Aye, sir," Zarah replied. "Got my spare team in Secondary Bridge already set."

Padraig nodded.

"Radio, status?"

"Probe is settling in and beginning to transmit now, sir," Nyssa replied. "Umbrella scan complete and perimeter settings in place."

"Excellent work, everyone," Padraig said. "Commander Schermer, you have the conn."

"All hands, this is Commander Schermer," Dana called over the line. "Stand by for insertion."

Padraig took a deep breath, then brought up a wider scan of the immediate vicinity, as well as Nyssa's Aetherial scanners. *Marrakesh* would be, as Maddox noted, in a sticky position if somebody else decided to become a problem this afternoon.

"Helm, down ten degrees and ahead ten percent," Dana called, her voice soothing and calm, which was exactly what you would want to hear when you looked up and saw a swirling vacuum into the depths of an ice giant over your head.

"Down ten. Ahead ten, aye," Zarah replied.

Marrakesh started down the ramp, clouds filling the horizon on the forward viewscreen, plus that monstrous, spinning toadstool in purple flecked with gold.

"Radio, passing through first pressure level now," Nyssa called. "Target is marked as third depth level."

"Roger that," Dana said. "Slow and steady, Helm."

From here, Padraig could see how the clouds did bulge some, but that was the storm itself rising above the surrounding colors like a plateau or a tor. That top still looked like a cylinder that had been shaved off with a plane, spinning inwards, then dropping sharply at the center.

"Second pressure level achieved," Nyssa said as the bridge fell to near silence.

"Helm, bring your planes up to four degrees," Dana ordered. "Reduce rotary thrusters to five percent, then prepare to dial them back to station-keeping as we come up behind the storm itself."

"Four degrees. Five percent forward power, aye," Zarah called.

Slowly, they overtook the storm, creeping along through the clouds.

"Pressure level three achieved," Nyssa called. "Still aft of the target location."

"Helm, bring your planes to level and drop speed to three percent," Dana ordered.

"Level and three, aye."

Now they were flying above the mess. The clouds were remarkably calm here, even though the altimeter said that they were only five hundred meters above the swirling indigo.

Anybody but Zarah flying, and he might be more nervous now. And it wasn't like the storm would badly damage the ship if they dipped into it briefly. The fear would be getting pulled down to the sorts of crush depths where the hull might not be able to hold, and the engines somehow weren't enough to drive the ship back up into orbit.

But Dana seemed confident. Padraig would rely on her competence.

"Helm, use positioning thrusters to lift us a few hundred meters altitude," Dana ordered. "Remain level otherwise and adjust forward velocity to track the storm from here."

"Stand by," Zarah replied.

Padraig could hear the stress in her voice, but the ship was drifting like a balloon now, in all the good ways.

"Elevation stable. Velocity stable."

"Excellent work, Helm," Dana said. "Radio, confirm my perimeter and a scan of nearby space before we proceed to the next phase."

"Nearby space is clear, Commander," Nyssa replied quickly. "Aetherial scanners show no unexpected behavior."

Padraig liked that term. *Unexpected behavior.* Everyone behaving themselves today as *Marrakesh* did something nobody else in the system could do.

And made them all watch.

"Helm, begin starboard roll one-eight-zero," Dana ordered.

"One-eight-zero, aye," Zarah replied.

Slowly, that cone turned into something like the Eye of God looking down at you, though it was still technically below them. Ominous as hell, though. And they weren't even over the center, but instead clear aft of the swirl, where the gases running vertical suddenly turned horizontal and began to curl inwards. They would pick up a tremendous amount of velocity as they got closer to that eye, but for now, it was more of a twisting ceiling, just out of reach.

"Wildcat crew, begin deploying your hose."

Padraig watched on a screen as the lines began descending, a tiny straw about to plunge into a violent sea.

"Gas lines at maximum hang, Dana," one of Dana's crew said.

Padraig let go the breath he had been holding as pressure on the hose began to climb and tank number seven began to fill.

"All hands, watch your gauges and your responsibilities," Dana said calmly. "It will take us about fifteen minutes to draw our fill, then we will reverse everything and back away the way we came. Congratulations."

Padraig nodded.

Something nobody else could do, which would just burnish his ship's legend, both here in Varfelis as well as with the fleet back home.

He was still worried about that other shoe dropping though.

125

31

———

Alex glanced up at his bridge once, then turned to study his force on the screen.

His, because he'd dipped into the bank and put a tremendous amount of credits onto the table for *Anteater*, *Velazquez*, and *Hermes Multistellar* to join him on a raid.

Back at Herli, there had been a lot of whispers after that. Rumors would be flying fast and heavy, and eventually someone would hit on the truth. The only question at that point would be if anyone believed them when they guessed that Alex Carson and *Hellhound* had become *Wronlori* privateers.

He'd deal with that problem tomorrow. Probably by going ahead and declaring himself the new governor of Varfelis Station and taking over the system as soon as all this was done.

Hopefully, the folks he'd been dealing with at *Wronlori* had been prepared to listen when he transmitted his mission plan. If they left him hanging out to dry after he destroyed *Marrakesh*, there wouldn't be much he could do about it.

He was already a pirate. Take the rest of the pirates and convince them to conquer and hold this region of space as a place, instead of feeding on it like parasites?

Weirder shit had happened.

In the back of his head, a clock struck some metaphorical midnight.

"Jeremy, open a joint channel to the other three so I can talk to Nicolau, Nyseth, and Velazquez directly before we head out," he ordered.

Two carriers with a total of either nine or ten snubfighters, depending on how well some last-minute repairs went on one of Velazquez's, damaged in a recent battle that had cost her her fifth.

One carrier shell with a pair of fourth-hand *Wronlori* gunboats that took up roughly two-thirds of the ship's interior when docked.

One armed revenue cutter.

And a lot of moxie.

Hopefully, it would be enough.

After all, he'd taken *Wronlori*'s money to do things like this, and Alex Carson liked to think of himself as a man of his word. He simply didn't give his word that often.

Or to that many people.

"Got all three, Alex," Jeremy interrupted his musings. "On your number two screen."

Alex switched views and saw the other three captains scowling back at him.

He nodded at their images and looked inside himself for the words.

"I'm not a rah-rah kind of guy," he began, aware that his own bridge crew would be hearing these words. As would theirs. "I'm doing this because that *A'Zedi* tugboat is softening up Varfelis Station to be taken over later. The years where we could grow fat as pirates might be coming to an end, if either *A'Zedi* or *Wronlori* decide to move this direction and set up permanent bases. At that point, we either have to answer to somebody's law, or move on to some other place where we start over. I'd rather crush the *A'Zedi* people, right here and right now. Rumors say that neither side of that war has the fleets to anchor and hold a place like Varfelis. Up until now, they haven't cared to try, either. *Marrakesh* looks like they want to change that."

He paused and studied faces. Still scowling, but softening some. Nobody wanted to grow up and act like adults. They wouldn't have become pirates if they did.

"We've had our differences in the past," Alex continued. "But we're all professionals here. And I had the money to hire you to help me drive *A'Zedi* out. You ready to go to work?"

"What happens after we blow them to hell?" Adrianna asked. "What stops them from sending a reprisal fleet?"

"Nothing," Alex admitted. "Except that *Wronlori* probably sends one as well in that case, and Varfelis becomes the front line in their war. Again, we'd have to pull up stakes, most of us. It's a risk I've had to come to grips with. Hopefully you aren't afraid of such risks yourselves."

From her scowl, she might have reached across a table and punched him. And he might have deserved it. But they were on their own bridges, and there was nothing she could do about the mild taunt except live with it.

Or run away in front of other captains and give him back all that money.

That would be the end of Adrianna Velazquez as a pirate. And they both knew it.

She nodded darkly at him, a promise of ugly words later. Or maybe some wild makeup sex. You never knew with that woman.

"Do we have to conquer Varfelis one of these days?" Porter Nyseth asked bluntly. "Seems like letting folks like Mendoza be in charge if outsiders are coming might be a bad idea."

"That's crossed my mind as well, Porter," Alex replied, skirting the truth. "Let's blow the hell out of *Marrakesh* first, then figure out what we might need to do to make some useful changes around here."

That mollified the man. For now. Probably end up having to make sure that *Hermes Multistellar* suffered some accident. Or got sabotaged.

Assuming that nothing terrible happened in the upcoming battle.

Alex could see the need to *accidentally* fire everything into *Hermes Multistellar* at short range, once *Marrakesh* was destroyed.

He'd wait to see how it all turned out, though.

Never count your chickens until they're hatched.

"Any other questions before we launch out?" Alex asked the three.

Grunts. Shakes of head.

"Okay then, Captains," he nodded. "All ships transition to Ghost-space and let's go hunting."

32

Nyssa had marked a couple of neighbors, back at Alanta. Folks with a lot of back-and-forth traffic that was encoded, but nothing interesting.

It had been the amount of traffic between two ships that didn't appear to be owned by the same folks, or to have anything in common.

One of them had followed *Marrakesh* to Annan. Long-range scans had confirmed that the other was still in orbit of Alanta.

Given the Captain's thoughts on potential piracy, Nyssa turned her attention to the boat called *Black Albatross* and started an in-depth study.

Primarily a cargo hauler. One of those ships configured as something of a mobile grocery store, hauling a lot of non-perishable goods and repair parts, so that miners could run lean in the field.

Dedicate every cubic meter to gas storage, which meant you didn't have as much for food and such. Normally, that meant you had to return to Varfelis Station pretty frequently, but then someone had started hauling the groceries into the field, along with a service garage.

Longer in the field wildcatting and processing, so you made more money when you got back to base.

It was an interesting economic adaptation to having a lot of gas and ice giants, and no truly habitable worlds growing crops in this system. Not even on the various moons.

Black Albatross itself wasn't all that impressive a ship. Mostly a giant cargo box with engines at the back, a flight and living deck above, and a huge volume of cargo like a grocery store taking up most of the space.

It helped, though, that the ship was open to automated, incoming transmissions, so folks could log into their computer, place an order for resupply, and pay without having to communicate verbally with the small crew aboard.

It left her options. Nyssa decided that they'd raised enough of a red flag with her to justify, so she unlocked all those other functions on her board and asked *Black Albatross* for a log-in. Automated systems. Not all that bright, because this place was close enough to the back end of beyond.

She put in all the information needed for *Marrakesh* to supposedly query their database for foodstuffs, then turned on the bits of snooping software that let her poke.

Nyssa was appalled at how easy it was to break in. At the same time, she was used to military-grade systems, at war with the enemy, including information security.

Black Albatross had almost no defenses against her.

Letting her paranoia run a little rampant, she inserted a few tools into their system and told them to grant her the highest level of access possible, while hiding her from the crew. Wasn't all that hard, as there was a level of computer operations below what most folks ever saw. Down on the iron and silicon itself, rather than bubbling up to where she might appear on lists of users.

All she had to do was tell the system to filter her existence whenever one of those higher-level functions ran a query. Child's play, really, given that *A'Zedi Intelligence Services* had handed her a toolbox and a training program in how to use it.

Nyssa went to work. First thing she did was transmit the complete inventory of *Black Albatross* back to *Marrakesh*, so she could go over it at her leisure later. Be one hell of a shame if she used a resupply run on one of *Marrakesh*'s shuttles to insert a boarding team and capture *Black Albatross*.

Kind of a reverse piracy move, if she found what she suspected.

And Cam and Trinh would both cackle madly at the opportunity.

Next, she dove into the flight system. Astrogation logs.

There. The brown dwarf. It even had a name, which it hadn't when she'd pulled everything from *Tyrannosaurus* before they sold it.

Herli Station. Apparently, there was a man-made object accompanying the brown dwarf through space. And a lot of pirates, looking at the supply runs *Black Albatross* had made there over the last year.

But then, little ships like this weren't important enough for anyone to worry about. They docked at Varfelis Station, loading up with supplies and paying cash, then ranging off on their various missions to resupply smaller places.

The literal definition of a tramp freighter lifestyle.

Even a pirate one.

Nyssa saved everything and looked up, realizing that she'd disappeared down a rabbit hole for nearly an hour. Commander Messier was in charge. Captain was in his cabin when she checked. Computer access showed that he was awake, so she pinged him.

"What's up, Taggart?" he asked, coming onto a visual screen instead of relying on audio.

"I've found some things, sir," she replied. "Normally, I'd come down there to brief you, but I need access to my console. Could I ask you to join me on the bridge?"

"Affirmative, Squire," he smiled. "Be right there."

Nyssa nodded as he cut the line, then leaned back. What other places should she poke?

Oh, standing orders. That might be good.

She meandered around their computer records for a bit before she found the captain's personal log and the woman's standing orders for her crew. The log would probably be a gold mine of data, but she didn't have time to listen to everything right now. Instead, she copied it to a secondary system and started compressing it for transmission back to *Marrakesh*. A slow trickle wouldn't get anybody's attention.

Standing orders: Track *Marrakesh*. Remain close enough to direct a ship named *Hellhound*.

Well, that was kind of obvious. Nyssa was about to start digging when Captain Boru appeared.

He must have jogged here from his cabin, but he wasn't breathing hard.

"What have you got for me?" he asked.

"*Hellhound*, sir," she said.

"Medium freighter that was in-system when we arrived," he replied immediately. "Remained somewhat close while we were in dock. I met their captain at the reception. Carson, I think was his name."

Nyssa blinked in surprise. But she supposed that sort of thing was what made him the captain.

She nodded.

"*Black Albatross* was ordered by *Hellhound* to track us, sir," she continued. "I have their flight logs showing that they went to the brown dwarf we've designated a pirate base. There is a thing there called Herli Station, according to *Albatross*'s records."

"Track us?" Captain asked sharply.

"Aye, sir," she said. "I'm in the process of pulling the captain's personal log for analysis, but that will take time, even with the tools I have at my fingertips. *Black Albatross* was in regular contact with a second ship that remained behind at Alanta."

"Show me your Aetherial scanner, Squire," he ordered.

Nyssa toggled screens and commands. The usual traffic of ships flying around, when you had the ability to listen out to a range of several light-years.

"Nothing out of the ordinary, sir," she noted.

His face was pensive. He reminded her of her own grandfather, when that man had a deep thought and was finding the vocabulary. She missed him. The rest of her family could largely get stuffed, but Grandpa Joe had always been a bright spot in her life.

"This smells like a trap," he said quietly.

"Should we capture *Black Albatross*, sir?" she offered.

"I'd love to, but then we'd have to admit to being something of a spy ship, Taggart," he smiled. "Can't have them guessing how we know the things we do. Or finding a way to thwart us later."

He paused, then keyed a line aft.

"Secondary Bridge. Messier."

"Chance, I'm bringing the ship up one alert status for now," he said. "Let everyone know that I'm expecting trouble to come over the hill pretty soon, but I have no idea when that will be, or who. Have the Q-Module teams remain at heightened alert as well. Wardroom can start delivering meals instead of them exiting the module to eat. Similarly, two command officers on duty at all times going forward."

"Found our pirates, finally?" Messier asked, excitement building in her voice.

"Maybe," Captain said. "Taggart cracked a couple of safes for me, so we know more than we did. I plan to take advantage of it. Also, make sure that whoever has Helm is ready to run like hell if we have to. Anybody gunning for us has done the math on a Tactical Transport, but they might decide to bring a big enough hammer to handle our improved firepower."

"Understood, Padraig," Messier said. "Writing up new standing orders now."

Captain cut the line and smiled at her.

"Continue your top priority to monitor that incoming flight vector corridor from Herli Station at all times," he ordered. "Specifically, because someone coming from that direction is likely looking for trouble, and if they're looking for us, that means they think they can take *Marrakesh*. Understood?"

"Aye, sir," Nyssa nodded. "I'll get all my people on it immediately."

"Excellent," he said. "Carry on."

She watched him exit and started typing up a new set of notes for her people.

Maddox might be *Marrakesh*'s Gunner, but Nyssa wondered if she was the one in charge of saving all their butts.

33

Padraig headed aft. He was off duty at the moment, but a captain was never completely relaxed. Always, there was something that needed doing.

He made his way to the B-Module and climbed up to the level where Kaitlin and Dana bunked. Every module that came with crew normally had the bottom few levels full of bunks, ascending to more important tasks as you went. The wildcatting team slept in small spaces tucked in around the big tanks and cracking refinery.

He found the lounge and noted the two women off in one corner, with a couple of sailors across the way generally ignoring them.

Padraig waved both women to remain seated as he joined them in a small booth.

"I've just been talking to Nyssa Taggart," he began quietly. "She's found a few things that have raised my concern."

Dana knew some of the truth about *Marrakesh* being on a scouting and survey mission that had more to do with espionage than exploration, so she merely nodded.

Kaitlin was fully briefed on what *Marrakesh*'s new mission was. She smiled knowingly.

"One of the ships with us is a spy for pirates, I believe," he said simply. "And from some things she's pulled out of their systems, I think they will be coming after us. Dana, what does it do to our maneuverability if we are fully loaded, instead of empty?"

"Not a lot," she said. "Other than the greater mass means that the engines have to work harder to accelerate us. We have connected the secondary lines that would let product from the refinery flow to the ship's fuel tanks if we had to. Some of the stuff we got at Alanta is refined enough to feed directly in a pinch."

Padraig nodded.

"I'm more concerned about timing," he continued. "Our schedule is reasonably well known, so someone wanting to ambush us should have a solid timeline."

"Should we move up the last run?" Kaitlin asked. "Dana and I were just discussing whether to take another run at that storm, given how valuable our first drink turned out to be when we ran it through the scanners. We could go in about thirty minutes if you wanted to surprise folks again."

"I think we should," Padraig decided. "Roust your people and have them get ready. We'll do the same thing as before, inverting over the calm tail of the storm and pulling in that last tankful. That lets us turn and hightail it to Varfelis Station, where we can off-load from the safety of their defensive armaments. Later, if someone wants to play, they either have to attack us there, or hope that they can chase us down on Ghostdrives, which I highly doubt, given most of the ships I've seen around here."

"Should we simply walk now, Padraig?" Dana asked. "I understand that the mission parameters were for a full load as a way of settling in around here long enough to scout what needed to be seen, but I think a risk to the ship might justify a change in itinerary."

"We have a legend to work against," he replied. "Cargo ship out surveying. Until someone actually attacks us, we're supposed to be entirely ignorant of what's coming. And there's no way in hell that a Tactical Transport like us should be reading another ship's logs, so I want to extend that ignorance as long and as deep as we can. Plus, we've spent all this time working on that cover. We still have a Q Module on the A-slot, if someone does want to start a rumble. That's a lot of firepower that hopefully nobody else has realized."

"You're the captain," Dana nodded. She turned to the two men across the way. "Jack, break's over. Roust the gang. We're going back over the storm as soon as Captain Boru gets his folks ready."

Padraig watched the two men scowl, nod, then start jogging for the stairwell. Dana smiled at him.

"Whenever you're ready, sir," she said.

Padraig rose.

"Good," he said simply. "One less thing on the list to accomplish."

He headed in Jack's wake.

Time to brief Chance, then bring the crew to full alert and go wildcatting one last time.

34

———

Padraig was buckled in. Locked in. Focused.

The rest of the bridge had picked up his energy and put their game faces on.

"All gun crews report ready for operations, sir," Maddox said. "Missile load-outs are heavy on Nines instead of Sixes or Threes, assuming swarms of smaller vessels rather than purpose-built warships in our future."

"Good call, Guns," Padraig nodded.

He turned to Nyssa.

"Long-range scan?" he asked.

"As expected, Captain," she replied crisply. "Maintaining visuals."

He nodded back. Upside down over an ice giant storm wasn't the worst possible place to fight a battle, but there weren't many worse on that list.

"Radio, launch your probe," he ordered. "Same settings as before."

"One thousand kilometers elevation, stable on the bullseye, aye," Nyssa acknowledged. "Launching now."

"Helm, stand by for insertion," Padraig ordered. "All hands, we are at full combat alert because I expect some of the neighbors to get chippy while we're doing this. You'll know about trouble as soon as I do, and I'd prefer if nothing happened today, but you are all at your stations because this is the riskiest moment of the entire operation. You have exceeded my already high expectations to date, so keep up the good work. Commander Schermer, you have the conn."

"This is Commander Schermer," Dana said over the line, no doubt standing next to Kaitlin and watching all the boards like a hawk with fledglings in the nest. "Helm, down ten degrees and ahead ten percent on rotary thrusters."

"Down ten, ahead ten, aye," Zarah replied sharply.

It helped that they'd already done this sort of thing seven times, once with the same storm that loomed before them on the viewscreen. Padraig didn't think it would become old hat this quickly, but it helped that they were facing the known, unlike that first time in the depths of Alanta.

"Radio, passing the first pressure level now," Bex Magorian called from the Secondary Bridge.

Padraig noted that Nyssa had handed off the local scanners to the other woman, and was locked intently on her Aetherial boards, watching the light-year distance. Bex was almost as good, and having the rest of the Radio crew trained on gas wildcatting just gave them extra skills for later. Whatever ship they ended up on, though he hoped that he'd be able to keep the best with him over a longer haul than most.

"Helm, bring your planes to five degrees and slow to seven percent," Dana called after a time.

"Five degrees down and seven percent, aye."

Marrakesh began to level off some. Still sliding down a ramp, but a shallower one now. And slower as they came up behind that monstrous storm, looming like a flat-topped, purple mushroom.

"Helm, bring us to zero plane and drop to four percent speed until you reach the marker I'm including on your screen, then drop to pursuit speed," Dana ordered.

"Zero and pursuit mode, stand by," Zarah answered.

Padraig noted how sure her hands were on her controls this time. That first, she'd been almost twitching, forced into rigidity by her focus. Now, there was a calm fluidity to her motions.

It was excellent training and would make her an even better officer on their next mission.

"We are stable," Zarah announced. "Standing by for inversion."

"Helm, begin your roll. One-eight-zero," Dana ordered.

The horizon rotated. Again, that first time it had been almost bizarrely frightening. He'd grown jaded as he noted how boring his crew made it seem.

As only the best did.

"Roll completed," Zarah replied. "*Marrakesh* is at rest and stable."

"Gas teams, begin your deploy," Dana called.

Padraig watched the line extend like a hummingbird's snout, then disappear into the purple maelstrom.

He had a small indicator on his side screen showing the tank filling as they began to pump. As before, it didn't take long.

"Radio, CONTACT!" Nyssa cut across all channels. "Four inbound targets on designated corridor. Presumed hostile until otherwise noted."

"Range and closure?" Padraig demanded.

"Two light-years and closing," she replied. "ETA twenty-four minutes and counting down."

Padraig noted his status board. Imminent combat shifted command back to him as soon as he took it.

"Gas teams, continue your draw," he ordered, taking command. "My boards show you should be filled in seven minutes. Immediately retract when you reach pressure, then lock everything down for combat operations. All hands, stand by to repel enemy vessels. Q-Module, stand by to unmask, but do not, repeat DO NOT show your colors just yet. I want that first salvo to be a complete surprise."

Somehow, he'd known it was going to go down like this. At least he had long enough to not be caught with his pants down.

Still, four suggested that someone thought he could attack a Tactical Transport and win.

They'd just have to see about that.

35

Zarah drew a breath and studied her boards. Flying inverted inside a planetary atmosphere was among the weirdest things she'd ever done, but after doing it a few times, she understood how to ride the winds like a glider.

Better, this pass over the storm was smoother, because she'd figured out where the cross winds died off at about five hundred meters vertical. The drag line tugged sideways, but she'd kept *Marrakesh* entirely above that after the roll. She was getting a feel for this sort of thing.

On her side board, Nyssa had filled in the enemy force. Four targets, moving in formation. Signature suggested they were all fairly small. Three medium freighters and something smaller.

It was the flying in formation part that probably had been the giveaway for Nyssa. That woman was smart.

"Gas team, retracting our line now," someone called over the line. "We'll be reeled and locked in four minutes."

Zarah nodded. Trouble wasn't here yet and wouldn't be for a bit after that.

She sat poised for the command to reverse the roll and blast out of the atmosphere, where they had space to maneuver against enemy vessels.

"Radio, what's the *Albatross* doing?" Captain Boru asked.

Zarah glanced over in confusion, but kept her mind focused on her controls. Captain was obviously up to something. And, after serving with the man long enough, she knew it would be great when it happened.

"Nothing, sir," she replied. "Nobody is watching their Aetherial scanners at the moment."

And just how the hell did she know that?

Zarah looked closer this time and realized that the woman next to her was sitting at the equivalent of a control board for a ship called *Black Albatross,* which was one of them that was in Annan's orbit but hadn't gotten close enough that Zarah had to worry about their maneuvering.

"Keep a watch, Radio," Captain said. "I expect that they might be about to transit to Alanta first, because they might not know we've left. Plot their inbound against that and let me know."

Oh, that made sense.

"Confirm course for Alanta, barring last minute deviations," Nyssa called.

Zarah turned her head to look directly at Captain Boru, drawing his attention.

"We're playing possum, Zarah," he smiled fiercely at her. "Keep things steady and level, inverted, then prepare to go to combat maneuvering when they arrive."

She nodded, a little perplexed. Being down here with that storm right below them greatly inhibited her ability to move around.

At the same time, she had everything lined up. No other ships above her in orbit, or ahead of her in orbit until she came about a quarter of the way around. She could open the throttles any time she wanted, limited only by friction of the thicker air around her.

"Wardroom, we'll be transitioning to combat maneuvers shortly," Captain announced in a cool, collected voice that almost sounded bored. "Your team will need to deliver meals to folks at duty stations for a while."

"Already got the trolleys deployed, sir," came the reply, but hadn't he warned everyone that they might be going to combat, even before the apparent bad guys had showed up?

Captain was up to no good. Zarah felt a grin take hold of her face.

This was going to be fun.

36

Nyssa had almost taken over *Black Albatross* and locked everyone out of the system but decided not to. Wouldn't be that hard to do. At the same time, the ship might suffer some problem if she did that, and they might not be able to fix it without their computers.

Still, it was armed, like everyone else around here. Looking through system security, she found a setting for locking and unlocking the plasma cannon that was located over the bow like a unicorn's horn. Currently, it was pointed directly aft down the centerline.

Nyssa went ahead and disabled it by putting the entire system into maintenance mode, then went through the user list and removing all rights to override those controls. Someone could still get in there and unlock it manually, but they'd also have to rotate and fire it by hand as well.

She seriously doubted that a group of civilian pirates were up to the task.

Then she turned her attention back to the attacking squadron. They were getting close enough to identify *Hellhound* at the rear point of a diamond, with two other ships roughly the same size on the wings. The smaller one was at the vanguard, so she supposed that it might be the most combat-worthy, though Nyssa had no idea what that might mean.

She routed everything to Captain Boru and Commander Messier to analyze and plan.

"Enemy warships still on course for Alanta," she called, mostly so everyone in the range of her voice would know what was up. "ETA four minutes."

Since the Captain had the ship-wide open, that would be pretty much everybody. It must suck, back in the kitchen, cooking without any idea what might be happening outside the hull. Or even outside the kitchen.

At least they'd have that much.

"Assume that they need about one minute to talk to their friend, reroute, and then charge this way," Captain replied. "Helm, we'll act surprised for a moment when they arrive, then begin maneuvering. Plot this course and prepare to engage it on my command."

Nyssa glanced over at Zarah's board and nearly swallowed her tongue in surprise when she saw what the captain had in mind.

And it would probably work, because he was going to do the front half of a forward roll, shifting off to one side of the storm itself, but using that swirly mess of purple to hide them from the pirates as they dove deeper into the gas beside it.

Assuming *Black Albatross* was in the middle for scanner sensitivity, the newcomers might not be able to track them if they went down a few layers into the deeper clouds.

And he'd had her put a probe into orbit above them, so even if they were blind below, Nyssa would be able to let everyone know everything happening, anywhere above Annan's horizon, which was most of orbital space from the height she had to watch from.

She grinned when she saw the look of pure delight on Zarah's face. They were almost back to Albany and that nebula, except that the enemy wasn't a Leviathan this time.

Instead, there would be a swarm of some sort.

It was her job to tell Captain Boru what he was facing.

Nyssa flexed her shoulders back and focused on her boards.

37

Alex had everything hot as they dropped on Alanta. Every pilot was in their craft, locked and loaded. Gun teams were prepared and had all had a potty break. They'd eaten and should be ready to transition directly to combat.

So, of course, *Marrakesh* wasn't here.

"Where?" he demanded, scowling at Gus on his screen.

"Annan," Gus replied. "*Albatross* has been tracking them. I'm transmitting your coordinates now."

That mollified Alex. Some. Hopefully, he still had surprise. There was no way for four ships to sail in an argosy without showing up on long-range scanners in the process, but they'd moved with speed.

And the lightspeed wave of their arrival would require several more minutes to get to Annan if they weren't on the ball checking the Aetherials.

Alex checked the file from Gus. He nodded and cut the line over to the other three.

"As you know, the target has moved," he announced. "But we've got their location as of twenty minutes ago, so we can come out right on top of them, launch all parasite craft, and attack. Helps that they are currently mining over a storm, so they might panic when we show up. Questions?"

Nobody had anything but growls and scowls for him, which was good.

Already, shit was going a little sideways, but it couldn't be helped.

"All ships to Ghostdrives and attack," he ordered.

Marrakesh, *I'm coming for you.*

38

Padraig watched the board showing the enemy vessels. It wouldn't take them hardly twenty seconds to jump here.

"Guns, unlock primary armaments and prepare to engage," he ordered. Probably unnecessary, but better than assuming. "Secondary teams, stand by to open your panels and unleash your surprise on our friends but hold until I give the word."

He studied the plot as those ships blinked up and out again, transitioning to Ghost-space for the short hop between giants.

"Radio, gun teams will need to know what we're facing, so be watching for secondary launches," he continued. "Scan those and feed Maddox size and vector for engagement. Helm, stand by to react in a panic when our friends arrive."

He paused, glancing at everyone around him. Calm. Cool. Collected.

He might not have considered something this crazy if these people hadn't gone into the nebula with him, but they'd proven their toughness. Their resilience.

There might be pirates coming for them, but Padraig had been expecting this for days. Planning for it.

He wasn't the one about to be surprised.

"CONTACT!" Nyssa called. "Four bogeys in diamond above us. Scanning now. Vectors confirmed and transmitted."

Padraig took a long moment to study, because his first response would set the table for the entire battle. *Hellhound. Hermes Multistellar. Velazquez. Anteater.* Weird names. Three cargo vessels and a cutter.

"Guns, the smallest one is probably best armed," Padraig said. "Missiles for the big boys but hold for maneuver. I want surprise."

"Locked and holding," Maddox replied. "Q-teams standing by."

"WARNING!" Nyssa followed up. "I have launches. Repeat, launches. Secondary craft from the rear three. Snubfighters and gunboats are launching. Prepare to receive fire."

"Helm, execute your roll, all ahead full," Padraig ordered. "Bring us down with the storm on our port, repeat PORT side as we go."

"Executing," Zarah replied. "Storm down our port as we come out. Everybody, grab on to something."

Padraig grinned. Artificial gravity fields meant that inertia as the vessel moved wasn't really a thing. At worst, you might get a little seasick watching these horizons roll, as your eyes and inner ear argued about which was real.

"Captain, do you want secondary craft or carriers killed when we emerge?" Maddox called.

Tough call.

Everyone was currently at short range, but that would probably not change, unless he decided to run sideways through the interior of the gas giant, daring them to chase him as missiles got lobbed up and out of the clouds Parthian style.

Marrakesh was tougher than the carriers. Maybe tougher than the cutter, kilo for kilo, if only because he couldn't bring himself to believe that pirates would maintain that sort of discipline.

"Go for the carriers," Padraig decided. "Drive them back or kill them if you can. We can always bounce out of here on our Ghostdrives to evade the little craft. And maybe the gunboats as well. Helm, what is your status?"

"Pointed straight down into the heart of a gas giant, Captain," Zarah replied with a voice that sounded like a laugh. "Coming around now. Guns, we are about to level off."

"Q Module, this is Captain Boru," Padraig smiled. "Unmask everything while we're hidden and start locking on your targets. I want a full spread of missiles shortly."

He didn't have many. Mostly, the Q-Module was particle beam turrets. Four defensive ones and two mighty Lancers for engaging someone at relatively short range with a big hammer. Like, say, the bad guys have sailed right up to you and demanded your surrender.

And while he had an additional six missile tubes to go with the six *Marrakesh* had, he only had twelve missiles total in the module to launch. Quick surprise to punch someone in the mouth, rather than stand off at medium range lobbing arrows at each other all afternoon, like a true Ship of the Line would.

They had to make it quick.

"Captain, we're ready to launch," Maddox said. "Range is so short that I've had to set the missiles to separate almost as soon as they come out of the atmosphere. None of them will be traveling all that fast on separation, nor will the fragments be able to spread out that much."

"Understood, Guns," Padraig replied. "Hold the second salvo from the Q Module in the tubes until everybody maneuvers some and we know how they will respond."

"Hold second launch, aye," Maddox nodded at him.

Padraig counted in his head, listening to his subconscious tell him when all those fighters should have gotten clear of their carriers. And be pointed the wrong way to add their plasma cannons to the defensive fire for what was about to happen.

"Guns, launch your full spread," Padraig ordered. "All twelve missiles as quickly as they can clear the tubes and ignite. Helm, give me a slight bow pitch up to help the missiles."

You couldn't actually launch twelve at once, because the exhaust from the prior one would interfere with the ones behind it. Instead, you kicked them free of the tubes with a steam catapult that literally threw them clear. Four seconds later, onboard gyros activated and spun the missile onto the new heading, then ignited the main engines.

He watched the first pair go, lightning bolts pointed up, riding twin pillars of flame into the sky.

Forty seconds later, all twelve were gone and racing away.

He turned to Zarah and caught her eye.

"Helm, bring your planes up thirty degrees," he said calmly. "Maintain full ahead and level us off to keep all turrets engaged with the enemy squadron."

She nodded.

"Up thirty and level flight, aye," Zarah replied.

"Let's go hunting, people."

39

Alex couldn't believe his luck. Then he wondered if those lazy shits on *Black Albatross* had been acting too suspicious, because *Marrakesh* immediately took off like a scared lizard, but DOVE INTO THE CLOUDS rather than trying to race to a corner where they might be able to get out from underneath his force.

If he stayed down there, *Hellhound* and friends could take potshots at him all day, even through the clouds, while maneuvering to keep him boxed in.

That had to be the dumbest thing Alex had ever seen.

"All fighters launched," Jeremy called. "Ten and two in the air. *Anteater* is moving into an attack position."

"Good," Alex nodded. "*Marrakesh* needs to be herded. Driven. Scanners, track them and make sure all the fighters have constant updates on where *Marrakesh* is headed. Gun teams, open fire."

"Alex, the clouds are gonna mess things up," Jeremy replied carefully. "Ionized plasma hitting those gases will degrade things pretty bad. That storm just makes it worse."

"All the more reason to get in there after him, then, isn't it?" Alex snarled. "Those lazy pilots think they're the king-shit around here. Time for them to earn that reputation. All fighters, dive and engage. Carriers, stand by for whatever missiles those folks think they can send our way."

Yavin appeared on a screen with a serious face.

"Hey, Alex," he said. "You want me going in with the fighters or staying out here with you?"

"You stay high, *Anteater*," Alex said. "He's got to come out at some point. Especially if he's got fighters gigging him in the ass down there. That'll be when you engage him."

"Gotcha," Yavin nodded. "Holding at altitude."

"Oh, SHIT!" Jeremy suddenly barked. "We got missile swarms coming at us. All ships, defensive fire immediately."

Alex checked the screen and shook his head in disbelief. Not only was *Marrakesh* not surprised, but how the hell had he launched… **twelve** missiles?

"Fire everything," he snarled. "Pilot, get us out of the way. Whatever you have to do!"

Alex shut his mouth as everyone went to work. Already, *A'Zedi* missiles were starting to fragment. Good and bad. They stopped accelerating when they did that. But now each one was nine pieces coming at him like a shotgun blast instead of a single bullet.

Hellhound had a pair of defensive plasma turrets. Both started jackhammering as quickly as they could fire and cool, like a lazy woodpecker hunting bugs. Tap. Tap. Tap. Tap.

"Stand by for evasive maneuvers," the pilot called.

Alex bit back another snarl. Anything he said at this point would just cause people to stop for a second and look at him, instead of concentrating on keeping them all alive.

The horizon suddenly dropped as *Hellhound* stood up on its hind legs and started accelerating.

Good, because that might get them out of the way of that missile swarm. Bad, because it pushed the whole squadron away from where *Marrakesh* was, letting the *A'Zedi* ship have space to get to orbit.

All the fighters were in the wrong place, too, having dived to chase, when it was obvious that *Marrakesh* had curled under that storm somehow. Under? Around? Whatever.

They had to have gotten under the shield, come about, and charged.

Charged? Shit.

"All fighters, come about and prepare to engage," Alex ordered. "*Marrakesh* is on the other side of the storm. Repeat, target has gotten around the storm from where you are entering. Circle up and over and prepare to engage."

Alex had been certain that the *A'Zedi* captain would run. Especially when he did, first thing.

Fucker had been playing possum. Waiting for *Hellhound* and friends to arrive.

And then fired off too many damned missiles.

What the hell?

Then he saw the first shimmer of starlight off metal hull as the big ship appeared below them.

40

Nyssa was watching three boards at once. Plus, Bex and Glen were tracking things and feeding them to her on the main image she was sharing with Captain Boru.

"Enemy fighters were going into the clouds after us but have been ordered up and over, Captain," she said. "I'm monitoring their communications, because they are not encoded."

He looked over at her briefly in surprise, like he couldn't believe it either, but she shrugged and he nodded.

How could she take advantage of this situation? There seemed to be one Marshal over there issuing orders for the full squadron. The captain of *Hellhound*. Alex Carson. In a calmer situation, she might have considered trying to brute force her way into *Hellhound*'s systems, but Captain was relying on her to keep everything tracked for Zarah and Maddox, and she didn't think that Bex or Glen were quite ready for that responsibility.

The probe had a good view of everything, and was above, looking down, so she could triangulate everything in the sky to the decimeter if she needed. *Marrakesh* was emerging on a flank, closest to a ship called *Velazquez* from the transponder code. Carrier, with four fighter craft it had launched.

They were concentrating on incoming missiles, which was smart, because the sky looked like an ancient, Persian manticore had let loose. Or a battalion of Swiss arbalesters.

Messy, in all the good ways.

Nyssa tracked vectors of sixteen nearby enemy vessels, as well as a half-dozen that might be in a position to help one side or the other. Nobody she knew well enough to request assistance, plus *Black Albatross*.

She paused and checked her pigeon. From the commands being typed into keyboards, they had finally discovered that she had locked them out of their gun turret.

Probably not worth sending a missile at them when it was an easy kill.

She kept that thought in the back of her mind, though, as everybody began maneuvering crazily.

41

Maddox had four heavy turrets at his command today. *Marrakesh*'s two heavy twins, fore and aft, plus the two Lancers on the Q. Everything would be at close range.

The ship designated *Anteater* had opened up with a pair of plasma cannons. Single tubes in turrets in the same fore and aft setting, but much lighter than Maddox had. Plus, they were defensive, trying to kill all his missile fragments. And doing a pretty good job of it, but the launch had been slow and early, so nothing was moving too fast to kill.

"All turrets, engage on target *Anteater*," Maddox ordered. "Defensive teams, we're facing three carriers and a cutter or corvette, so there may not be enemy missiles. Stand by and track on your vectors. I might cut you loose to engage warships or fighters at your long range."

He smiled at the cheers and hoots on his private channel. Those folks were keyed up, but usually didn't get to hurt anyone, because proper battles were at ranges where even the heavies were pretty dispersed by the time they impacted.

Here, the Lancers were going to pack one hell of a punch.

"Forward turret, I have lock and engaging."

"Q-2, engaging."

"Q-1, firing."

"Aft turret, we're maneuvering badly. Shifting targeting to *Velazquez*."

"Tube One reloaded with a Six. Ready to fire."

"Tube Two, same here."

"Tube Three, I've got a hang. Skip me this sequence while we get the missile aligned."

"Tube Four, armed and ready."

Maddox nodded. It happened. Especially when maneuvering madly and firing everything. A line would kink or a missile would not want to line up properly to go into the launcher. Good teams had a whole host of tools at hand, from hammers to levers to hoists. Whatever was needed to get it into place.

Worse was when something pinched or broke and you had steam everywhere. Still, his gunners were well trained, and he'd taken some extra time to have inspections done on all his tubes, knowing that they were likely to be used this week.

Maddox looked at his targeting screens and noted flashes of light on *Anteater* where bolts of plasma were impacting. That ship looked military, so he had to assume decent armor protecting the interior. The others were all civilian cargo ships. Tin cans.

Velazquez rotated ten degrees downbow and started to roll when the aft turret scored a hit. A cloud of plasma erupted, but that looked like hull shattering under the heat, rather than a penetrating blow breaking something internally.

Nyssa waved a hand at him, causing Maddox to look over at her.

She tapped a spot on her screen and Maddox looked at his echo.

Yup. About time those yahoos got back into the battle.

"Aft turret, rotate and engage gunboat-1," he ordered. "All turrets, both gunboats have missiles on external racks. Stand by to receive incoming."

"Aft turret, we'll see about that."

Maddox laughed. Forward Gun Turret was the prize position for his crews. Unless you were running away from somebody, there would be many times when your maneuvering meant that the aft turrets couldn't come around far enough to engage. Today, they had an absolute plethora of target options and were milking it for all they were worth.

"CONTACT!" Nyssa yelled. "I have two, repeat TWO launches from the gunboats. Incoming missiles tracking."

"A-battery, got them lined up."

"C-battery, same here, as long as we hold this line."

"B-tracking number two. Going to have to fire through an enemy fighter to engage. Shucks."

"D-battery, permission to fire on an enemy warship until somebody small wants to play?"

"Affirmative, D-battery," Maddox replied. "Stay sharp, but there are no friendlies until they surrender."

Freaking shambles, that was what it was. But Captain had really messed with their plans twice so far. Once by diving and drawing the fighters out of position. Then again when he'd charged at a corner firing everything and causing enemy gunners to have to concentrate on missile fragments.

Looked like they had a chance here.

42

—————

Padraig watched more than a dozen vectors as Nyssa updated them three times per second. Loading a Tactical Transport was frequently a job handled in three dimensions, so he'd trained himself to see all those vectors simultaneously and understand where folks were going as they turned, twisted, and accelerated.

Twelve missiles had turned into something like eighty, scattering fragments between Sixes and Nines. Slow-speed meteors passing through the enemy squadron. Only problem was that slow speed let their gunners kill them.

He was fine with that, because it had let him get clear of the clouds and start moving around where *Marrakesh* would have a serious advantage on smaller, softer ships.

"Helm, bring us around three-four-zero and cut speed twenty percent," Padraig ordered, bring the bow around to port and aiming *Marrakesh* right at *Hellhound*.

A year ago, Zarah Halloran would have looked up at him in surprise, even for a moment. Today, she simply nodded and kept typing.

"Three-four-zero, and decelerating, aye," she called. "What about our engagement plane, sir?"

Padraig looked at the screen and saw what had caught her eye.

"Agreed, Helm," he said. "Down five degrees to get us below them a bit, then level off."

"Down five and level, aye."

Marrakesh, like most ships, had the turrets on the top of the long, flat hull. No particular reason that they couldn't be on the bottom of the hull, other than the way humans liked to operate their equipment. Ships of the Line tended to put things along a flank. Smaller target for the enemy, but you had to maneuver more carefully, or roll a lot, when you needed to change targets.

Cruisers weren't expected to sail in line astern when fighting. Here, getting lower meant that all of his turrets were better able to engage. And the missiles were launched sideways from the flanks anyway, so they didn't care where you were in three-dimensional combat.

"Radio, how's *Velazquez* doing?" he asked.

"Turning away, sir," she replied. "That hit hurt, but the ship itself is merely a carrier. They have one big twin plasma cannon turret for weaponry. All their firepower is in the fighters they carry."

"Understood," Padraig said. "Guns, let's ignore *Velazquez* for now and take out their flight wing."

"Roger that," Maddox said. "Gun teams, transition to tactical defense mode."

Padraig nodded. Bow on, he presented a smaller cross-section for enemy vessels to shoot at. And the fighters had to keep maneuvering if they didn't want to fly right into a plasma bolt, so they couldn't be that accurate.

"A-battery, engaging missile. They are fragmenting early, so prepare for rapid fire."

"B-battery, that fighter got in my way. Now engaging missile fragments through the wreckage."

Padraig tuned the rest out. Two gunboats with a total of four missiles weren't a threat unless they got exceptionally lucky, with his folks prepared and firing.

He turned his attention to *Anteater*. Battered, but still fighting. *Marrakesh* was sending missiles down in pairs now instead of salvos, and *Anteater* was doing an excellent job dispatching them. Shame those folks had decided to be pirates, because that was some truly professional sailing.

Still, they were pirates.

"Guns, stand by for an overload salvo on *Anteater*," Padraig ordered.

"Overload, sir?" Maddox confirmed, looking up from his boards.

"Give them the rest of the Q-Module missiles, Guns," Padraig said. "Plasma can deal with fighters and missiles. I want their escort crushed."

"Aye, sir," Maddox nodded. "Q-teams, everyone lock on *Anteater* and give him your other barrel. Stand by for rapid launch salvo."

The hull jarred once and threw Padraig against his restraints.

"What was that?" he asked.

"*Anteater* getting in one last punch, sir," Chance called from aft. "That and one of the gunboats got lucky with a plasma hit forward and low. Damage control parties dispatched."

He nodded.

It was a battle. Things happened. Especially when you had that many guns and missiles going back and forth.

Padraig checked his boards, but nothing seemed out of the ordinary. The bow was twice as heavily armored as the rest of the ship specifically for fighting like this. Minor penetration and a few shorts on his board, but very little important stuff was up there. Mostly spare parts and raw metal to be fabricated into other things.

Crew quarters and generators tended to be aft, where they were safer.

"Q-Module, fire as you bear!" Maddox ordered.

Padraig watched the other six missiles launch as quickly as they could, plus two from *Marrakesh*, everything aimed at *Anteater*. Didn't matter if they were an escort. He'd be facing nearly fifty multi-ton arrows passing through his flight corridor in the next minute.

"Guns, how are we doing on fighters?" Padraig asked.

He had the same numbers as Maddox in front of him, but a captain was focused on the entire battle, rather than any one facet. And Maddox was sharp.

"They're going for a swarm, sir," Maddox replied. "Not a lot I can do but keep up defensive fire."

Padraig nodded. That was the risk, going bow on with them. Their guns tended to be fixed on a centerline, save for the two gunboats with their turrets.

At the same time, they could slow down as they got alongside, riding their gyros to pour fire into *Marrakesh*'s flanks.

"Helm, plot me a course that takes us directly under *Hellhound* at close range," Padraig ordered. "All ahead full."

"Intercept and charge, aye!" Zarah yelled grandly, sounding like a buccaneer about to draw her cutlass and swing across the gap on a rope.

Modern piracy didn't work that way, but he could still scare the hell out of Alex Carson.

"Maddox, reserve the Lancers for *Hellhound*," Padraig ordered crisply. "Everyone else engage anything that they can hit, including the two big turrets. Am I clear?"

"Aye, sir," Maddox replied. "Q-Module, lock the Lancers to *Hellhound*. Everyone else engage as you bear."

Padraig watched the swarm charging. His four short-range plasma turrets, plus four on the Q-Module. Hell, even the railguns were starting to take plinking shots at this range. The big turrets couldn't swing fast enough to track a fighter, but just having those massive bores pointed at you ought to cause the pilots to flinch away.

Anything to lessen their fire over the next sixty seconds.

43

———

Alex turned to stare at Jeremy.

"Repeat that," he snarled, thunderstruck.

"*Marrakesh* is coming right at us," Jeremy repeated. "And accelerating."

"Are they ramming?" he screeched.

"Negative," Jeremy shook his head. "Current path has them passing below us at less than one thousand meters distance."

"METERS?" Alex demanded.

"Aye."

"Get us the hell out of the way, then," Alex ordered. "Pilot, up and accelerate. Immediately!"

"Oh, shit, we just lost *Anteater*," somebody called over the raucous noise.

"Lost?" Alex yelled back. "What happened?"

On the viewscreen, there was a ball of expanding plasma where his fourth ship had been ten seconds ago.

"They overloaded him with missiles," Jeremy replied. "At least three hits, almost simultaneously."

Shit.

Shit shit shit shit shit.

"And *Marrakesh* is coming for us next?" he asked, mostly to confirm the inevitable.

Jeremy nodded, grimace seemingly etched into his face with a hammer and chisel.

The hull suddenly shook with some impact.

"Heavy plasma fire from *Marrakesh*," someone yelled. "They've ranged and locked."

Shit.

He turned to his First Mate.

"Get us out of here," he ordered. "Pilot, all ahead with everything you've got. Maximum evasion, then transition to Ghostdrives as soon as you can."

"Run?" Jeremy asked.

At that moment, *Hellhound*'s twisting brought *Velazquez* onto the main screen. Possibly crippled. Possibly dead. He wasn't sure.

Alex Carson locked eyes with Jeremy Luna.

"You want to die instead?" he asked. "Right now, it's every man, and woman, for himself."

Jeremy nodded.

Better to be marked a coward than to die when the cops showed up to arrest everyone.

Hellhound began to flee.

44

Nyssa watched the battle unfold.

Anteater was gone. Simply vanished in a ball of spare parts and plasma gases expanding.

Velazquez hadn't maneuvered since that first hit, so maybe it had been hurt more than she'd expected.

Hermes Multistellar wouldn't be carrying one of its gunboats home, as the forward turret had crushed it with a lucky hit. The ship itself hadn't been hammered too hard yet.

Hellhound reared back like they were starting to run.

She saw a really rude opening.

"Bex, take over scanners," she ordered, then ignored any response.

Black Albatross wasn't particularly close but had flown in their direction as soon as battle had started. And still hadn't figured out what she'd done to their turret. Nor had they told anyone they were experiencing technical difficulties.

She reached a hand into their system and brought their one turret live, setting it to automatic engagement and designating *Hellhound*'s squadron as their targets.

It opened fire. Not much more than a flashlight from this range, but the sudden squawks of surprise on the open comm in her ear brought a smile to her face.

"Taggart, is that you?" Captain asked.

"Affirmative, sir," she laughed.

"Excellent work," he said. "What's *Hellhound* doing?"

"Accelerating and climbing, sir," Bex replied from aft. "Vector suggests he's about to go to Ghost-space to escape us."

"Status on the remaining two carriers?" Captain asked.

"One down, one largely unhurt."

"Helm, stand by to pursue *Hellhound*," Captain ordered. "Engineering, I need to chase someone who wants to get away from us. Whatever you need to do to get me ready."

"Everything already on standby and waiting for the order, sir," Chief Engineer Jareth Ahearn replied laconically. It almost sounded like he was laughing as much as Zarah was.

"CONTACT!" Bex yelled. "*Hellhound* is running. Tracking on Aetherial scanners."

Nyssa locked *Black Albatross* out of their own communications circuits so they couldn't even tell their friends what was going on and left the guns firing.

Best they could do at this point was run, before the remaining two ships sent their flight wings over to kill him for the betrayal.

"Helm, pursuit mode NOW," Captain ordered.

Nyssa nodded and turned back to where *Hellhound* was trying to get away.

Trying.

45

___

Padraig felt the ship lurch as Zarah got them into Ghost-space after Carson. He'd be willing to let the other two limp away. *Hermes Multistellar* might not have either gunboat, from the way things had shaken out in the last fifteen seconds. *Velazquez* might not fly without a few days of repair.

Anteater didn't exist anymore.

Piracy in the Varfelis system had just gone markedly down for the foreseeable future.

"Status?" he called, looking over at Nyssa.

"Target is up and away," Nyssa replied. "Current speed Mark Four point Five. Point Seven. Point Nine. Stable at Mark Four point Nine."

"Helm, lock in and zero down on him," Padraig ordered. "Maneuver for a Ghost-space shot with all guns."

You could fight in Ghost-space, moving at FTL speeds, because you were technically in another universe that closely mirrored this one. Except for the ability to go really fast.

At the same time, nobody had ever figured out how to mount Ghostdrives on a missile and make it an effective weapon here. You chased the enemy vessel, getting close enough that you could start taking potshots at them from under one light-second range.

The physics got entirely wonky, but it was possible to score hits. And with the way Ghost-space worked, a hit frequently ejected the target ship back into the real universe, stranding them for several minutes or even hours while they reconfigured everything to try again.

You had that long to stop, turn around, and engage them in real space, then maybe you were back to chasing them again.

That stupid Leviathan had kept up with *Marrakesh* at Six point One. Lucky for him that *Hellhound* couldn't match that.

He'd been afraid that they had some extra engine power hidden in there, letting them get up into the range of those racing yachts or priority transports where Mark Ten was common.

You ain't getting away from me, Carson.

"Helm, how close is his course to Herli Station?" Padraig asked as things stabilized.

"Almost dead reciprocal, sir," Zarah replied.

"Understood," Padraig said. "I need him finished off before then. Guns, start your plot. Expect to use everything."

Maddox gulped audibly and nodded. He'd never done something like this, mostly because you hardly ever did. Once a ship came off the Ghostdrives, it took time for them to cool and reset. Ergo, you could run somebody down.

But *Marrakesh* hadn't been in Ghost-space in days, so all the drives were ready to go. And he was willing to bet that they could recycle faster than a pirate anyway.

Professional sailors.

Pity *Anteater* probably had no survivors. Those folks had impressed him.

The rest were career criminals with no redeeming qualities.

"Range?" Padraig asked, mostly to keep his people from squirreling in too tight.

"Nine light-seconds and closing smoothly, sir," Nyssa replied. "Course has stabilized on Herli Station. Is he running for their guns?"

"I'm guessing it was panic initially," Padraig replied. "That was why I had Zarah set the course I did. A bull charging in an arena. At that point, he has to go somewhere, and I doubt that there are any other places anywhere close where he might find somebody willing to protect him from our guns. Ergo, Herli Station. I would prefer we knock him down before he gets there."

"Estimated intercept in forty-five seconds," Zarah said calmly, no longer that crazed buccaneer with a knife in her teeth.

Probably.

"Guns, stand by," Padraig ordered.

175

<h1 style="text-align:center">46</h1>

Alex watched the scan. It wasn't possible, but it was.

Marrakesh was running him down with ease, and there was nothing he could do about it.

Worse, they hadn't stayed to kill *Hermes Multistellar* or *Velazquez*. Instead, they'd ignored those two and immediately set out in pursuit.

He'd figured that he'd get something like a twenty- or thirty-minute head start. Maybe not enough to disappear off their Aetherial scanners, but far enough away that they decided not to chase.

Instead, that Captain Boru had annihilated *Anteater* and was coming for him, leaving Porter and Adrianna to get away.

Assuming that they could. Those last sixty seconds had been utterly brutal.

Nobody had told him that they had battleship firepower hidden in there.

And that was likely to cost him his life.

Alex looked up and saw Jeremy scowling at him.

Alex could do the math. Maybe they decided to kill him and hope that *Marrakesh* would show mercy in capturing them?

Varfelis wasn't big on the death penalty, and there'd be no reason to haul him back to an *A'Zedi* world for punishment.

"Should we change flags?" Jeremy asked in a quiet voice that most of the bridge crew probably didn't hear over their own chatter and noise.

Alex considered it.

Technically they were a *Wronlori* privateer. He had the paperwork back in his safe, but that had been intended for any *Wronlori* warship that happened along and wanted to do something about piracy.

And he would definitely be captured and hauled off to a prisoner of war camp.

Would *Wronlori* trade him home? Or disavow him entirely, wash their hands of *Hellhound*, and let him rot in an *A'Zedi* prison for the rest of his life?

Still beat dead.

Dead meant you had no more options.

"Do it," Alex ordered. "Lower the black flag and swap the transponder to show us as a *Wronlori* warship."

"Will they even see it in Ghost-space?" Jeremy asked quietly.

"Anything is possible," Alex replied. "At this speed, they'll kick us out pretty quickly. We'll have a little time for them to review. Then we'll surrender."

The rest of the crew groaned, but nobody drew a weapon and killed him. Or even threatened him.

"Hey, you scumballs," Alex roared. "If we're sailors operating under cover as part of *Wronlori*'s war, they have to take us prisoner and intern us. That's way better than being hung from the neck until dead I hope you will agree. Get it through your fool heads that every damned one of you is a patriotic *Wronlori* freedom fighter and that you expect to be traded home at some point. We'll deal with the rest from inside wherever they send us. Now, shut up and back to work."

It sucked, but dying was his only other option right now.

Marrakesh wasn't about to let him get away.

47

Padraig watched the two ships close inexorably in Ghost-space. Outside, space was passing under their keels at nearly five light-years per hour. Inside Ghost-space, they were less than a single light-second apart.

"Flight stable and vector-matched," Zarah called with a deep sigh.

"Guns, go to work," Padraig ordered.

"Radio, give me a hard scan of physical space on *Hellhound*'s flight corridor," Maddox called.

"On your number four screen, Guns," Nyssa replied instantly, like she'd already known Maddox was about to ask. Excellent teamwork.

Maddox studied the results and nodded.

"All gun teams, take five seconds and zero your weapons for the first salvo on the coordinates I have designated, then lock them in place and turn on your gun cameras. We'll take a shot, then estimate what real space is doing to deflect the bolts, then shoot again. Signal green when ready."

Padraig watched not just the four big turrets light up, but the eight smaller ones as well. Hell, the railgun teams were probably bitching up a storm that they couldn't engage, but the ranges only looked small on screens. They were still several hundred thousand kilometers separating the two ships.

"Stand by to fire," Maddox said solemnly. "All guns fire."

Instead of each taking potshots, all twelve turrets went off at once.

Six on the Q Module, plus six twins on *Marrakesh*. Eighteen bolts, fired functionally simultaneously in a narrow salvo.

And Maddox had had them locked down tight.

The squall line of plasma rain missed low and to the right of *Hellhound*, rippling away and fading.

Maddox nodded and made some adjustments on his screen. Then added one final twist after a moment.

"All guns teams, adjust your aim point as indicated and mark your status green," he said, pausing and drawing a deep breath as he waited. "Stand by to fire. All guns fire."

Whatever that last tweak had been, it was seemingly the critical one. Padraig watched the giant space hammer slam into *Hellhound* like a maul breaking rocks.

"CONTACT!" Nyssa called. "Target is out, repeat OUT, of Ghost-space. Estimated coordinates transmitted."

"Stand by for maneuver," Zarah called.

Padraig smiled. He'd known some captains who would have demanded that those two officers not react until he'd specifically ordered them to, introducing lags of as much as five seconds to each step of the process and making it that much harder to lock down on where *Hellhound* had gone to ground.

He had trained them to take the initiative in moments like this.

Today was why.

On his screen, the closest stars suddenly slid sideways as Zarah cut her speed and slewed the bow around hard in a tight circle, like a skier being pulled behind a boat on the surface of a lake.

Quickly, they circled back to the coordinates, then dropped back into real space. And Nyssa had been paying extremely close attention, as they only ended up about half a light-second from the target when they appeared.

"Radio, give me a hard scan of the target," Padraig ordered. "Helm, ahead half speed and prepare to back us down to zero. Use your discretion to get us close then bring us to rest. Do not wait for my order to slow and stop. Any order I give will probably be to chase, so if they run, start after them immediately. Am I clear?"

"Close and intercept, aye," Zarah replied. "Prepared to chase if they run, aye."

Padraig nodded.

"Oh, shit," Nyssa muttered, then looked up at him with eyes like a frightened deer.

"What's their status, Taggart?" he asked.

She paused and drew a breath, straightening her back and sitting up a little straighter.

"Enemy vessel has suffered a catastrophic failure, Captain," she said firmly. "I'm showing two major components at present, with most of the forward third of the vessel as one piece, and the upper half of the middle third being a second."

It took him a moment, then she showed it on his screen, and Padraig nodded.

"All hands, stand by for rescue operations," he ordered, keying the ship-wide again in case someone wasn't paying attention. "Flight deck, get both your birds in the air with medical teams and security personnel to take charge of prisoners immediately. Damage control teams, stand by to move to EVA operations as Radio tracks down enemy sailors adrift in suits. Move it, people!"

He leaned back and studied the screen. Zarah was moving quicker, but more delicately, nosing *Marrakesh* right down as close as she could get it to the ruptured hull of *Hellhound*. Or rather, the biggest piece, which was the bow.

"Engineering, what happened, in your professional estimate?" he asked.

"Somebody kicked their ass, sir," Jareth replied. Padraig was about to snarl an obscenity at the man when the man continued, so Padraig let him have his joke. "I'm guessing a fuel line ruptured close to an oxygen tank and filled a couple of blow-out chambers that didn't vent like they should have. Ignition introduced torque along the lines of the blow-out chambers, and again, it was held inside instead of vented. Bad maintenance, most likely. The rest of the tanks aft went in a sympathetic chain reaction, so all of Engineering is pretty much reduced to plasma at this point, though there might be some smart folks back there who managed to get into suits beforehand and got clear of the hull when it went up. Mid-section probably doesn't have any survivors, but we'll have to board to confirm. Overshock probably squished them, if the pressure was sufficient to rupture the hull like that.

Forward looks reasonably intact but running without any life support. That sufficient, Padraig?"

"Thank you, Jareth," Padraig replied, mollified. "Nyssa, transmit that to all hands so they know where to expect survivors. Flight Deck, put a team aboard the forward section first, then see if you can kill their tumble and forward velocity with your engines so *Marrakesh* can dock and get survivors off as fast as possible. Security teams, you're on. Radio, see who you can contact and bring them up to speed. I doubt anybody over there has any fight left in them."

He leaned back and considered his options.

They were pirates, so technically he was within his rights as captain to leave them here to die, but Padraig never wanted to be that guy. Or to have that kind of reputation. Stories of what had happened at Annan would get around, so folks would know *Marrakesh* was more dangerous than she appeared. As would rescuing all the survivors off *Hellhound*'s corpse.

Flight of Fancy launched first. On his screen, Air Boss Walt Rafferty was flying it himself, but Padraig wasn't surprised. And the man was the best pilot aboard, so he'd be the one Padraig wanted trying to handle *Hellhound*'s bow.

He keyed a line aft.

"Wardroom. Quirke."

"Chief, we're standing down from combat operations," Padraig said. "Lots of coffee will be necessary shortly, as well as food and comfort for a bunch of rescued sailors."

"Already in process, Captain," Landry replied evenly. "Been waiting for your call."

Yes, he supposed they had back there.

He had a good team.

And now he had a bunch of pirates to deal with.

48

———

Cameron was on point. Trinh was right behind her, both of them armed to the teeth and ready to shoot first, then deal with the survivors. If there were any.

Walt was up front flying.

"Stand by to dock," the Air Boss called.

Flight of Fancy bumped once, then rattled as he dialed in the locks.

"Reminder that we are without gravity over there," Walt said. "Emergency lighting is on, from what I can see through a couple of portholes. Stand by in the airlock."

She was suited up. As was her whole team. Four more gunners and two medics, mostly because they expected to have to load *Flight of Fancy* up as quickly as they could locate people and triage them. Nobody expected pirates like this to have much more than an autodoc.

Nor would she really trust any doctor who was reduced to serving on a pirate vessel.

The airlock started to cycle. Folks on *Hellhound* should had recognized the sounds and rumbles of docking, but Cam supposed that they might be kinda busy at the moment.

Still, she had her pistol pointed at the center of mass on the guy standing in the corridor revealed. He didn't have magnets in his boots like her, so he was floating with one hand on a stanchion.

Wasn't wearing a suit, either. She wondered how many suits they might have had available. Pirates, and all that.

Her external mic and speakers were live.

"Rescue teams," she announced. "You going to be a problem?"

"Negative," he said. "Jeremy sent me aft to get you. We're done."

Wasn't a name she knew, but Cam didn't care. She seemed to remember a note somewhere of an Alex Carson as captain of this boat.

"You folks ready to surrender?" Cam asked, not moving yet.

Out of the corner of her eye, she could see Trinh's pistol appear around her hip. Probably a couple more over her shoulders, if her crew had kicked up from the dock where they could float high enough to see over her hundred and eightty-eight centimeters.

"Via, yes," the man replied, exasperated. "This way."

He kicked off and headed forward along what looked like the port half of a pair of corridors running the length of the ship. Smoky haze filled the air. Most of the lights were out, but there were emergency lights here and there. Not a lot of crew visible.

The pirate got a certain distance, then caught a post and paused, looking back. Cam was walking on magnets instead of swimming, in case she needed to move quickly. Her team were strung out behind her, with the last two walking backwards or crabwise as they went.

Fellow got to a bigger hatch and pushed the button. It took a little doing to slide sideways, because it felt like the hull had torqued pretty good.

Lots of smoke billowed out of the room that was revealed. Man floating coughed a couple of times but went ahead and dove into the haze.

Cam followed her pistol to the hatch and looked in.

Yuck.

Wasn't a bridge hit, because they still had pressure in here, but more than half the stations had caught fire or exploded in the last twenty minutes. Fires were all out, and she could see a dozen bottles of fire extinguishers floating in one corner inside a cargo net.

Quick count said four dead people, under tarps and tape, and four live ones.

Smaller guy had been doing something on a station that was still intact. He looked up at her, nodded, and rose slowly.

"Alex is dead," he announced. "I guess that means I'm in

command. Jeremy Luna. We need to go back to his cabin and get all his paperwork, so we can claim prisoner of war status."

"You shitting me, Jeremy Luna?" Cam asked. "You folks are pirates."

"According to Alex, we were operating undercover as a *Wronlori* privateer, *A'Zedi*," he snapped tiredly at her. "Before he died, he told me everything was aft in his safe. He's dead, but I've been too busy here keeping shit from coming apart to go look."

"Well, you're my prisoner now, Luna," Cam replied. "My orders are to evac your crew to *Marrakesh* soonest. How many crew do you have?"

He shrugged, eyes not entirely focused.

"Crew was thirty-seven originally," Luna said. "I got four here. Rest were aft or are too injured to respond to calls, plus whoever got in suits and escaped."

Cam picked out one of Luna's men.

"You, go with this woman," she said, pointing to Trinh. "Trinh, you take the med teams and two and start clearing cabins for evac."

"Got it," Trinh said, moving.

Cam went ahead and holstered her pistol for now. She could always quick-draw and fire, but these boys looked like they didn't have any fight left in them at this point.

"*Marrakesh*, this is Farrell," she said, switching to the main line. "I have a status update..."

49

——————

Padraig was aft when Farrell brought her main prisoner to *Marrakesh*'s airlock. Walt Rafferty had been able to smooth things to the point that Zarah had easily docked, so Padraig had been able to get crew members back and forth quickly.

Sixteen survivors, from thirty-seven crew listed. Four in critical condition and not expected to survive. Five more in medical in descending degrees of severity. Seven ambulatory, including the apparent First Mate, with Captain Carson dead in battle.

Luna was a small man. Maybe one hundred and seventy-five centimeters, and a bit pear shaped. Worn down, from the shock etched onto the man's face.

"Captain Boru, First Mate and acting Captain Luna," Farrell introduced him. "Jeremy, this is Captain Boru."

Jeremy?

The man nodded.

"Let's do this thing," he said tiredly to Farrell.

She nodded and headed back into the ship. Padraig noted that Trinh Hoàng was close, but nobody else.

Chance had command of the last of the rescue operations, but at this point they were down to whatever salvage was worth the effort. They'd rescued everyone left alive.

The bow of *Hellhound* was smoky and running now on power from a feed line run through the airlock. Life support was air blown in from *Marrakesh*, with all the close filters marked to be changed next week. If not sooner.

Hellhound was a pirate ship. Dark, dirty, worn with age.

Battle damage hadn't helped, but it had been a civilian cargo ship off the assembly line, and folks had added things with cutting torches and welding lasers since then, so bits stuck out at odd angles and different colors.

Luna led them to a hatch and keyed it open with a code. Farrell leaned in and jacked it once with a shoulder when it balked halfway. Probably the hull had pinched. She didn't seem surprised.

"Captain's quarters," Luna announced as he entered.

Cramped.

Bed built into the long wall. Desk with a sloped surface emerging from a short wall. Closet with rumpled clothing. Chair at the desk that looked comfortable enough to sit in and read.

About a quarter of the total deck space that Padraig had on *Marrakesh*. He wondered if this was just a crew cabin. It had that feel.

Gravity was on because *Marrakesh* had added power. Things had fallen to the floor or been strewn about. Luna ignored them and moved to a safe set in the wall above the bed, kneeling on it to reach.

Padraig wondered about security, but he had two of the most dangerous women on his crew in here with him, and Luna didn't feel like a threat.

The man entered a code into the keypad, then pushed a button and it beeped, opening about a centimeter.

Rather than pull it the rest of the way, Luna turned to Farrell quizzically.

"Go ahead, Jeremy," she said quietly, like she was talking to a wild animal on the verge of spooking.

Luna shrugged and pulled the safe door open.

"Oh, he did have a pistol in here," the man said, surprised.

"I'll take it," Farrell said, stepping close and reaching over the shorter man's shoulder.

Farrell was about two centimeters taller than Padraig, and he was pretty tall.

Disruptor. Pretty good shape. She tossed it to Hoàng and went back to her prisoner.

Luna pulled out several envelopes of various sizes, shapes, and colors.

"This is probably it," he said, holding up something with a *Wronlori* naval logo on the outside. Then he surprised Padraig by handing it over, putting everything else on the bed and standing up. "I either need some coffee, if you expect me to stay up for a while, or some whiskey, so I can relax."

"Trinh, your prisoner," Farrell said. "Take him aft and get him taken care of. Thank you, Jeremy."

The man nodded absently and brushed by Padraig in the cramped space as he exited.

Padraig opened the folder and started quick scanning the contents. Then he paused, cursed, and pulled a comm from his pocket.

"*Marrakesh*. Taggart."

"Nyssa, drop whatever you are doing," Padraig ordered. "Grab an engineer and a tool kit. What you did to *Tyrannosaurus*, I need you doing to *Hellhound*. The parts you might need could be floating in space. Hopefully, they haven't been destroyed."

"Datacores are designed to survive crashes and explosions, sir," she replied.

"Find it," he said. "Retrieve it. Immediately. This is your highest priority until I say otherwise. Out."

He cut the line and stuffed the device back in a pocket, turning to Farrell.

"He specifically said that they claimed to be a *Wronlori* privateer?" Padraig asked.

"Freedom fighter was the term Carson used a few times, sir, but yes," Farrell nodded. "What did you find, sir?"

"Alex Carson was a spy for *Wronlori*," Padraig said simply. "*Hellhound* was a deep-cover operation, according to his orders, to create a piracy problem in this region. I have bank records. Naval orders. Notes on his real name, in case he needed to convince someone. The works."

"And the datacore?" she asked, excited.

"Probably has everything we could possibly want to know about *Wronlori* military movements and plans for this entire sector, going back at least three years, when he recruited a crew of cutthroats and pretended to be a pirate, Farrell," Padraig said. "If Nyssa can find the rest, we've just earned our gold star for this quarter's efficiency report."

She smiled proudly.

He couldn't say more. There were only four people on *Marrakesh* who knew the truth about his own deep-cover orders: Chance, Kaitlin, and Nyssa.

But yes, when he got this information back to Permanent First Secretary Gelashvili, she would most definitely smile.

50

Padraig was a bit surprised to be called to the Permanent First Secretary's office without Nyssa along this time, but he supposed that other folks would be wanting to debrief his radio officer to a depth of detail that would make Padraig's eyes cross trying to follow.

He'd come up as a Gunner, rather than Radio, in his time. Knew how those things generally worked, but he also knew that Nyssa Taggart could do things that maybe a handful of people in the entire fleet could replicate.

And most of them likely also worked for Madame Gelashvili.

"Sit," she said as he entered her office and they found themselves across that immaculate desk.

He did, watching her not like a mouse watches a hawk, but maybe something close.

She'd asked for a spy. Turned him and his crew into a spy ship. Padraig doubted that anybody had been prepared for this.

"The man you know as Alex Carson was indeed a deep-cover *Wronlori* agent, Captain," she began, possibly in the middle, but he hadn't gotten the impression that Mariami Gelashvili wasted a lot of time on idle talk in her life. "What you have found as well as done at Varfelis Station has, at a minimum, set *Wronlori*'s plans in that area back at least two years. Possibly four or more, because we intend to leak selected bits to trusted merchants heading that way."

"Ma'am?" he asked, unsure where all this was headed. "Implications?"

"If spun correctly—and I have the right kinds of spin doctors on staff here—we ought to be able to drive an ugly wedge between the folks in that region and *Wronlori* itself."

"If you really wanted friends, you'd go crush Herli Station, ma'am," he offered.

"Oh?" she brightened. "It wasn't on our immediate plans, Boru. Why should *A'Zedi* put forth that level of effort, so far from any operating bases of ours?"

"*Wronlori* was funding a lot of that piracy, from the bits Taggart did share with me, ma'am," he said. "In destroying *Hellhound*, *Anteater*, *Velazquez*, *Hermes Multistellar*, and *Black Albatross*, we've made a serious dent in the amount of pirate firepower that region can call on. If we hit them again in the short term, before more pirates can move in to replace them, we might be able to limit if not annihilate piracy in that region. And it will make the local merchants better disposed to *A'Zedi* ships, military or civilian, that might call at Varfelis Station or nearby systems later."

He leaned back, aware that he was offering strategic advice to someone at the very top of the command chain. Unsolicited, to a certain degree.

She watched him with hawk's eyes.

"It would need to be at least a battlecruiser, Captain," she offered back. "If not a Ship of the Line."

"I might suggest a small squadron of frigates, mistress," he countered. "Perhaps with an older light cruiser as a flag commander. I doubt that the station itself will have a lot of firepower, but likely relies on pirate ships and defensive batteries. Missile frigates could stand off and threaten to annihilate them with shards from a safe distance. Once they surrender, we evac the crew and blow it in place. No more pirates."

"And not turn it into some sort of forward operating base?" she asked shrewdly.

"Far outside our normal zone, ma'am," he replied. "You'd almost have to drop a major fleet out there to hold it, and I'm guessing that we're stretched too thin at this moment to do it. Maybe in five years, if *Wronlori* doesn't see the error of their ways."

She leaned back and smiled, but that smile hardly made Padraig feel better.

"What if I were to tell you that my advisors came up with almost exactly that analysis, Captain?" she pressed.

"You've got good people and I got lucky, ma'am," he nodded.

"I have very good people, Boru," she nodded. "Including you and Taggart. Fleet is making arrangements to quietly slip out and crush that station, though they may arrive and blow it up rather than rescuing everyone afterwards like you did."

"Those are orders that can be given, sir," he snapped to. "I'd prefer not being that sort of captain, myself."

"And that, right there, is why I value you so much, Boru," she said. "You catch more flies with honey than vinegar. I've read the reports of Lead Expert Farrell and how she managed to turn enemy pirates into helpers."

"Nobody wants to suffocate and freeze when the life support finally dies, ma'am," he offered.

"Exactly, Captain Boru," she replied. "Farrell acted that way because you had created that as a ship's culture. Going above and beyond what was expected. That makes you valuable."

"Just doing my duty as I see fit, First Secretary," he said.

"Keep doing it," she nodded. "Did you have any questions for me?"

Padraig stopped and considered it.

"Not at the moment, ma'am," he said.

"Then dismissed, Captain," she said. "We'll be in touch, once your crew gets some time off."

He rose and started for the hatch.

"Oh, and Captain?" she called him to turn around. "Good job."

"Thank you," he said. "I've got an amazing crew."

"You do, Boru," she nodded. "That you do."

READ MORE

Be sure to read the rest of the Operation Marrakesh series!

https://www.knottedroadpress.com/product-category/science-fiction/
operation-marrakesh

ABOUT THE AUTHOR

Blaze Ward writes science fiction in the Alexandria Station universe (Jessica Keller, The Science Officer, The Story Road, etc.) as well as several other science fiction universes, such as Star Dragon, the Dominion, and more. He also writes odd bits of high fantasy with swords and orcs. In addition, he is the Editor and Publisher of *Boundary Shock Quarterly Magazine*. You can find out more at his website www.blazeward.com, as well as Facebook, Goodreads, and other places.

Blaze's works are available as ebooks, paper, and audio, and can be found at a variety of online vendors. His newsletter comes out regularly, and you can also follow his blog on his website. He really enjoys interacting with fans, and looks forward to any and all questions—even ones about his books!

Never miss a release!

If you'd like to be notified of new releases, sign up for my newsletter.

http://www.blazeward.com/newsletter/

Buy More!

Did you know that you can buy directly from the KRP website?

https://www.knottedroadpress.com/shop/

Connect with Blaze!

Web: www.blazeward.com
Boundary Shock Quarterly (BSQ):
https://www.boundaryshockquarterly.com/

ABOUT KNOTTED ROAD PRESS

Knotted Road Press publishes dynamic fiction set in exotic locations and unique non-fiction voices in genres such as autobiography, business, cookbooks, and how-to. Our authors cover a wide range of genres including science fiction, fantasy, mystery, literary, and poetry, appealing to all readers. We offer both DRM-free ebooks and print books for a global readership.

Knotted Road Press
www.KnottedRoadPress.com
www.KnottedRoadPress.com/Shop